"I Guess This Is Good-bye."

"It is." Lander paused. "If that's what you really want."

"We settled this already."

"You can leave." He shifted closer and covered Juliana's hand with his, preventing her escape. His breath stirred the curls at her temple while his voice murmured seductively in her ear. "You can get out and we'll never see each other again. Or you can stay. Think about it. We can have one evening together before we go our separate ways. No one has to know. I can arrange that. No media attention. No spotlight. Just a man and a woman doing what men and women have done throughout the ages. One night, Juliana."

Dear Reader,

Welcome again to the imaginary country of Verdonia and the princes and princesses who people it and offer such rich material for their various love affairs. I want to thank the Harlequin Romance readers who have followed me to Silhouette Desire. And a special thanks to Desire readers for giving The Royals trilogy a try.

This book was a special one for me because I love dealing with issues of trust—or the lack of it. I've always felt that learning to trust completely and utterly, is what love is all about. This book also gave me the opportunity to introduce the hero for my fourth Desire book, *The Billionaire's Baby Negotiation,* available in September, and I hope you fall in love with him as much as I did. He's a special one.

Please come visit me at my Web site: www.dayleclaire.com. I love hearing from readers

Best,

Day Leclaire

P.S. Don't miss next month's conclusion of The Royals, *The Royal Wedding Night.*

THE
PRINCE'S
MISTRESS

DAY
LECLAIRE

Published by Silhouette Books
America's Publisher of Contemporary Romance

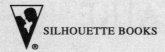 SILHOUETTE BOOKS
®

ISBN-13: 978-0-373-76786-1
ISBN-10:   0-373-76786-2

THE PRINCE'S MISTRESS

Copyright © 2007 by Day Totton Smith

This edition published by arrangement with Harlequin Books S.A.

Visit Silhouette Books at www.eHarlequin.com

Printed in U.S.A.

Books by Day Leclaire

Silhouette Desire

The Forbidden Princess #1780
The Prince's Mistress #1786

*The Royals

DAY LECLAIRE

Day Leclaire is the multi-award-winning author of nearly forty novels. Her passionate books offer a unique combination of humor, emotion and unforgettable characters, which have won Day tremendous worldwide popularity, as well as numerous publishing honors. She is a three-time winner of both The Colorado Award of Excellence and The Golden Quill Award. She's won *Romantic Times BOOKreviews* Career Achievement and Love and Laughter awards, the Holt Medallion, the Booksellers Best Award, and has received an impressive ten nominations for the prestigious Romance Writers of America RITA® Award.

Day's romances touch the heart and make you care about her characters as much as she does. In Day's own words, "I adore writing romances and can't think of a better way to spend each day."

To Jada Andre, who can't be thanked often enough.
You've been an unbelievable help.

One

Mt. Roche, Principality of Verdon, Verdonia

Prince Lander Montgomery gripped the phone and spoke in a low, forceful voice. "You owe me, Arnaud. You've been in my debt for years. It's time for you to pay up, and I have the perfect way you can do it."

"I don't owe you a damn thing," Joc snapped. Even from half a world away his voice was as clear as though he stood in the same room. "You and your cronies made my life hell at Harvard. You're lucky I haven't tried to even the score. But now that you've taken the time and trouble to remind me of those good ol' days, I may reconsider."

Lander glared in disbelief. "Payback? After all this time?"

"Why not? When you have as much money as I do,

payback can be a real bitch. A fact you'll soon discover firsthand, Your Highness."

"You have a convenient memory. I'd almost think you'd forgotten about graduation night." Lander paused. "Not to mention the promise you made."

Joc snarled a curse. "I was out of my mind when I made that promise."

"No doubt. But still, you made it. Or doesn't the infamous Joc Arnaud honor his promises? Given your background, I thought honor was everything."

There was a moment of dead silence and Lander wondered if he'd pushed too hard. Then, "What do you want, Montgomery?"

Lander fought to disguise his relief. Years of practice maintaining an impassive facade came to his rescue and was reflected in the calmness of his voice. "I want to discuss a business proposition. I'm throwing a charity ball this Saturday. I understand you'll be in the vicinity."

"If you consider Paris in the vicinity."

"It's a hell of a lot closer than Dallas. Where should I send the invitation?"

"Corporate headquarters. And make it two. There's someone I'd like to invite to your little shindig."

"I'll courier them to you today."

"You never did say…" A hint of curiosity climbed into Joc's voice. "What do you want from me?"

Lander smiled in satisfaction. When it came to Arnaud, curiosity was a good thing. A very good thing. "Not much. I just want you to save Verdonia."

She was late. Unforgivably late.

Juliana Rose mentally willed the cab to hurry, to cut through the heavy traffic overflowing the streets of

Verdonia's capital city of Mt. Roche and reach her destination while she could still enjoy what remained of the evening's festivities. Even if she made it to the palace within the next five minutes—highly unlikely—she didn't doubt for a single moment that she'd be the last guest to arrive.

Peering through the window, she struggled to see how much farther they had to go. In the distance the palace of Mt. Roche topped a nearby hill. It gleamed silvery gold beneath an early June moon, its graceful turrets and glittering stonework reinforcing its fairy-tale appearance. A hunger built deep inside, a hunger to believe in fairy tales and happily-ever-after endings, even though she'd learned long ago that such things were impossible—at least for her.

This was her very first ball, a reward for all her charitable work for Arnaud's Angels. The fact that the fates were busily conspiring to prevent her from enjoying the fruits of her labor simply underscored her suspicion that some things were never meant to be. Besides, wasn't it considered a major no-no to arrive after the royal family? Would they even let her in? Or would she be turned from the door before she had the chance to peek inside? Well, she'd find out whether they'd let her in soon enough. And if they didn't… She shrugged philosophically. She had a briefcase full of work back at her apartment and a dozen potential candidates who would benefit from Angels' benevolence.

As the cab turned onto the winding approach to the palace, Juliana struggled not to fuss with her hair or tug at the scrap of beaded silk that bared more of her breasts than she found comfortable. Instead she folded her hands in her lap and cleared her mind by silently working her way through a complex mathematical equation. She'd stumbled across the trick as a child, starting with simple multiplication tables to calm herself whenever she'd been upset. Since then, she'd refined the technique, increasing the level of difficulty until it took all her focus and concentration to work her way through the problems. To her relief, the exercise worked, easing her tension and allowing her to regain her poise.

At long last the cab pulled through the palace gates and cruised slowly around the sweeping circle to an entryway as elegant as it was imposing. "Lion's Den," the driver announced in near perfect English. But then, most Verdonians were fluent, since it was their second language. Even the children she worked with spoke English as well as she spoke Verdonian.

"Why do you call it the Lion's Den?" Curiosity compelled her to ask.

He shrugged. "Prince Lander is the Lion of Mt. Roche."

"So you call the palace the Lion's Den?"

He acknowledged her amusement with an answering grin. "Well…perhaps not to His Highness's face."

"No, I imagine not."

With a quick word of thanks, she added a generous tip to the fare and exited the cab. She could practically hear the clock ticking a frantic warning that time was passing, but she refused to rush, choosing instead to soak in the beauty of her surroundings. Normally she wouldn't have dared attend an affair like this. But she was in Verdonia, a small European country that rarely gained media attention, and far—she hoped—from the intrusive focus of the paparazzi. No one knew her real name here, that she was an Arnaud. Instead, she'd been using her first and middle name. She was just Juliana

Rose, charity worker, invited to the ball as a generous afterthought.

Tonight she had an opportunity she'd never experienced before. Tonight, she'd be able to cut loose from her conservative image and allow a tiny piece of her natural personality to take over. To shine as hot and brightly as she dared without worrying about who was watching or taking note of every word she spoke, or dress she wore, or man who danced with her.

Tonight she could be herself and damn the consequences.

Footmen lined the great hall, unobtrusively directing her along the corridor. As she suspected, she was the only guest not yet in the ballroom. The spiked heels of her sandals fired off a rapid tattoo against the endless expanse of marble flooring. With every step she felt more and more like Cinderella, though if she were fortunate her Elie Saab gown wouldn't dissolve into rags on the stroke of midnight any more than the cab she arrived in would revert to a pumpkin with a mouse for a driver.

Passing between huge Doric columns she found herself on a large curved landing overlooking the gathering. A majordomo guarded the wide staircase that led downward into the mass of glittering partygoers. She paused to absorb it all, to savor every single aspect of this moment out of time. Flowers of endless variety and hue overflowed urns and vases, filling the room with a lush, heady scent. Elegant French doors were thrown wide, allowing a soft warm breeze laden with the advent of summer to filter through the throng, and causing the candles that lit the room to flicker and dance. Eventually her attention drifted to the staircase leading downward. And that's when she saw him, positioned at the foot of the steps as though he'd been waiting for her.

He was tall. Even standing a full story above him she could tell his height was impressive. He wore his black tux with casual ease, his chest and shoulders a virtual wall of immovable masculinity. Thick, wavy hair swept back from his face, streaks of sun-bleached blond competing for supremacy over the rich nut brown.

She could see his chiseled features were striking, with high arcing cheekbones and a strong, square jaw that warned of a stubborn nature. But it was his mouth that fascinated her the most. It sat at odds with the hard, forbidding lines of his face and jaw. That mouth betrayed him, the lips full and sensuous and perfectly designed to give a woman pleasure. There was a volcano of passion brewing beneath that mountain of calm control, passion requiring only a single spark to ignite an explosion. The knowledge stirred a secret smile, one that faded the instant she realized he was watching her.

While she'd been studying him, curious and unguarded and exposed, he'd been busy returning the favor. Their gazes locked and held for an endless moment. Heat pooled low in her belly, lapping outward in ever-increasing demand. Never in all her twenty-five years had she experienced anything quite like it. She'd heard of women who'd been struck by that sort of sexual lightning bolt, had even scoffed at the possibility, but she'd never believed it possible.

Until now.

Now, she was faced with an urgent demand she could no more restrain than deny. She knew this man. Oh, they'd never met. But somehow she recognized him. Connected with him on some primal, instinctive level.

For instance, she knew with every fiber of her being that he was a strong man. Powerful. A leader. And she knew that he'd taken one look at her and decided he would have her. He wanted her, wanted to sweep her into his arms and carry her off to his own private lair. To lock her away and possess her body, heart and soul until he'd had his fill of her.

The knowledge almost had her stumbling backward. Pride kept her locked in place. He wasn't the first of his kind she'd had to sort out. She'd spent her entire life dealing with strong, powerful men. They were nothing but trouble. They demanded full control and considered everyone and everything within their world a challenge to either conquer, absorb or destroy.

She also knew that if she were smart she'd turn around and flee the palace. The safest recourse open to her was to hail a cab and return to her apartment where she could hide herself in precious anonymity. There was only one problem.

She wanted him, too.

Flight or confrontation? Rationality or insanity? She hesitated for a telling second before lifting her chin. To hell with it. She'd never before thrown discretion to the winds. Tonight would be her one chance and she intended to seize it with both hands. Gathering up her silk chiffon skirting, Juliana started down the steps and toward whatever fate the gods decreed.

Prince Lander Montgomery stood at the bottom of the staircase leading to the ballroom and stared at the vision standing, still as a statue, in the shadows on the landing above. She was absolutely magnificent—statuesque, with the sort of figure capable of making grown men weep. Her skin rivaled the color and beauty of the white lilies that dotted the floral displays, and set off hair that at first appeared brunette. But then she stepped into the light, and flames erupted from the darkness, smoldering like hot ruby coals. It reminded him of the fire that hid in the richest of Verdonia's world-renowned amethysts, the spark of hidden red that would heat the blue and purple to a blistering inferno and had made the unusual gems some of the most coveted in Europe.

She wore an elegant silver gown, the low-cut corsetted bodice and capped sleeves forming a triangle that framed her neck, shoulders and breasts. Her gaze drifted across the ballroom and a smile broke free, chasing the aloof expression from her face and completely altering her appearance. In the space of a heartbeat she went from cool and regal to warm and vibrant. And then she glanced in his direction.

Heaven help him, it was one of the most intimate looks he'd ever received—open and direct, and as arousing as a lover's caress. A matching hunger consumed him, a ravenous need. One look and he knew he had to have her. It didn't matter why. It didn't matter how. He'd never felt such urgency before, had never felt on the bitter edge of control. Not over a woman. He'd always been the one in charge, the one to set the terms. It was his right and one he'd taken full advantage of.

Until now.

She handed her invitation to the majordomo and then swept down the staircase toward him, crystal beads glittering with every movement. Lander found himself blessing whichever designer god had created her gown, mesmerized by the way the silver material clung to her shapely hips before flaring outward. Layer after layer of tissue-thin skirting lifted and fluttered to show off a spectacular pair of legs.

It was like a scene straight out of *Cinderella*. Except this prince had no intention of falling madly in love. In lust, perhaps. Hell, definitely. But love belonged right where Cinderella found it—in a fairy tale.

Reaching the final step, she hesitated. She continued to stare straight at him, her eyes the color of gold-flecked honey. He read barely suppressed excitement there combined with an inner fire that burned so fiercely he could feel the scorching heat from where he stood. It drew him, stirring an uncontrollable desire. It also roused the predator in him. He wanted to have her focus that iridescent gaze on him and only him, to discover the cause of her suppressed excitement. Free it. Just as he wanted to free her inner fire and bask in its searing intensity.

A ripple lapped outward among the nearby guests, warning of gathering interest. Verdonia was a small country, the people attending tonight's charity gala familiar with one another. This was the first ball since his father's death, a traditional affair Lander had known his father would have wanted them to hold, despite being in mourning. And into the darkness this exotic stranger had appeared, cutting through their grief with fiery brilliance. It wouldn't be long before one of the un-attached males—or even a few of the attached ones—approached her.

Before that could happen, Lander closed the distance between them. She was tall. In her four-inch heels she easily hit six feet. "Welcome," he said simply. "I've been waiting for you."

Wariness clouded her eyes and she retreated a pace. "Do you know me?"

Odd question. Did she think they could have met in the past and not remember each other? Not a chance. "No, I don't know you. But I hope to change that."

Her relief was palpable, a fact he found intriguing. "My mistake," she murmured. Her husky accent held the unmistakable sultriness of the American south and tugged at something visceral deep inside him. "I thought perhaps we'd met and I'd somehow forgotten."

"No. It was my rusty attempt at a pickup line." Lander's mouth twisted. "It would appear I'm seriously out of practice."

For some reason his admission succeeded where the line hadn't. "In that case, you can practice on me. I promise I'll go easy on you." She leaned forward and lowered her voice. "I wasn't certain they'd let me in if the royals had already arrived. I don't suppose you know the proper protocol? Is there someone I should speak to? Apologize to?"

As a pickup line it worked far better than his had. "Prince Lander, for instance?" he suggested with a teasing smile.

To his surprise, alarm flared. "Definitely not him. I'm just here for the party, not to hobnob with any luminaries. In fact, the first one I see will be the last, because I'll be out the door in two seconds flat."

He fought to keep his face expressionless. How interesting. Unless she were the best liar he'd ever met, she didn't recognize him. That had to be a first. Nor did she want to know him, which meant keeping her far from anyone who might give his identity away.

"As it happens, I do know the proper protocol," he

responded in a grave voice. "You've missed the receiving line. Fortunate, since it's damn boring. But it's a serious lapse in etiquette to arrive so late. You'd be smart to get onto the dance floor as quickly as possible before someone notices and has you removed."

Alarm flitted across her face before she caught the wicked gleam in his eyes. Her smile flashed, filling her expression with a sweetness as unexpected as it was appealing. "I don't suppose there's anyone here who knows how to dance?"

He made a show of looking around before shaking his head. "I've seen these men in action. It's not worth the risk. Considering how late you are, it's either me or the dungeon."

Her eyes widened and she managed to appear suitably shocked. "The dungeon, huh?"

"I'm afraid so." He shrugged. "Blame it on Prince Lander. He takes this whole I-am-lion-hear-me-roar stuff pretty seriously."

"So it's either dance with you or be dragged off to the dungeon. Tough choice." She pretended to consider. "I suppose I'd be safer in the dungeon."

"True." He held out his hand. "But safe isn't always as much fun."

"And rarely does it give us our heart's desire." She came to a swift decision. "I'll dance with you."

With that, she accepted the hand he offered. The instant they touched it was as if time slowed to a crawl. Outside of their tiny world, sound grew muffled. Light dimmed. Movement paused. Her fingers were long and supple within his, revealing both strength and softness. He found he didn't want to release her, didn't want to sever the connection between them. Rather he wanted to draw her closer, to taste her, inhale her, touch far more than just her hand.

Her breath quickened as he continued to stare, the pulse leaping at the base of her throat. Her lips parted in anticipation and in that twilight of stillness he could feel the heady rush of scented air as she swayed toward him. It was all the agreement he needed, the most subtle of feminine signals giving him permission to take what he wanted. He tugged her into his arms, and just like that, time clicked back into its normal rhythm. He had enough self-possession—barely enough—to turn his actions into the first steps of the waltz the orchestra was performing.

Sweeping her onto the dance floor, he circled the room. She fit beautifully within his hold, her height making her a perfect match. He kept the dance simple and basic. She followed him without hesitation and he increased the intricacy of his movements, delighted when she matched him step for step.

Her scent tantalized him, and he drew it deep into his lungs. "What's the perfume you're wearing? I don't recognize it."

"You wouldn't. It was a gift from—" She broke off self-consciously. "It's a special blend, number 1794A."

He couldn't help but wonder who had given it to her. A former husband? A current lover? Aw, hell. The fact that he cared was a bad sign. A very bad sign. He gritted his teeth, searching for something to say that would distract him from the futile path his thoughts were taking. "What have you named it?"

She tilted her head to stare at him blankly. "Named it?"

"You're kidding, right?" Okay, now he was distracted. "You have a perfume blended just for you and you haven't named it?"

She shrugged, disconcerted. "Was I supposed to? I didn't realize."

"Most women would have." Hell, most women would have named the perfume after themselves.

"I'm not most women."

"So I'm discovering." And he found that fact fascinating. "I just realized we never introduced ourselves. Tell me your name."

"Juliana Rose." The mischievous expression in her eyes accentuated the burnished gold flecks. "And shall I call you Prince Charming?"

He shot her a swift, suspicious look, but couldn't detect so much as a hint of guile. "There are those who'd disagree," he replied, sidestepping the question.

"That's because you threaten your partner with the dungeon if she refuses to dance with you. I don't suppose there's any chance of a tour of the palace?"

"I could show you the gardens. But the rest will have to wait for another night."

Her smile flashed. "In other words, we're allowed in the gardens but the main part of the palace is off-limits."

"Something like that."

"And here I thought you were an influential man with unlimited power."

He stiffened. "What makes you say that?"

"Instinct."

"Do you know me?" he demanded, throwing her earlier words back at her.

In response, she eased away from him, distancing herself. A wash of cold air cut between them, while wariness stole the open warmth from her expression. "Should I?"

"Verdonia is a small country."

"I'm not Verdonian."

"No. American, if I'm not mistaken. And you still haven't answered my question."

"Okay, fine. Yes, I'm American." It wasn't what he'd asked, and she damn well knew it. The contest of wills was brief. It took a strong person to stand up to him. And though he believed Juliana possessed unusual strength, it was no match for his. With an exclamation of annoyance, she conceded, "No, I don't know you. As far as I'm concerned we're two strangers who have the opportunity to enjoy a single evening together before going our separate ways."

"Instead of happily-ever-after we indulge in happy-for-one-night? Is that why you came here?" he demanded. "So you could meet a stranger and spend an evening with him? Is that the current American euphemism for a one-night stand?"

Instead of reacting in anger she grew more remote, more regal. "I came because I received an invitation to the ball," she said with devastating simplicity. "And I have to settle for a single evening because that's all I've been given. After tonight I return to real life. You see, I discovered long ago there's no such thing as a happily-ever-after ending. One night at a royal ball won't change that."

"Then I suggest we make the most of the one night we have together. Have you ever been to a ball before?"

"No." Her voice dropped, the wistful quality underscoring her words hitting him low and hard. "At least, not to anything like this."

"I'm surprised."

"Really? Why?"

"Because you look like you belong. You act like it."

"I don't," she replied shortly.

"I'm not so certain. You're wearing a couture gown. Your shoes are handmade and would have cost the average citizen·a month's pay." He could sense her dismay and wondered at it. "Shall I continue?"

"If you must."

"You walked into the palace as though you were a Verdonian princess. Proud. Confident. At ease with your surroundings. It tells me that even if you've never been to a royal ball, you're accustomed to elegant affairs."

"I may have been to one or two," she conceded.

She'd aroused his curiosity. "Why is it so difficult for you to acknowledge that fact?"

"Because it's in my past. This gown?" She swept her hand over the silk chiffon skirt. "The shoes? Even my invitation are all gifts. If they hadn't been I wouldn't be here. It's not a lifestyle I enjoy. Not any longer."

Lander didn't have a single doubt there was a man involved in that decision. Had she been some wealthy man's mistress? A plaything for the rich and powerful? Any man would have been delighted to have such a woman gracing his arm, not to mention his bed. The thought infuriated him, rousing a primitive possessiveness he'd never before experienced and one he fought to restrain. What did it matter who or how many men she'd been with? Right now she was in his arms. And if he were extremely fortunate, later tonight would find her in his bed.

"So you've chosen to leave this sort of lifestyle behind," he managed with impressive lightness. "Or you have until now."

"Well…" He caught a hint of self-mockery. "It *is* a royal ball. What woman could resist indulging in that sort of fantasy for one night?"

The dance ended and she stepped free of his embrace before he could prevent it. "Then allow me to make your night as special as possible."

His offer gave him the excuse to touch her again, to take her hand and gather her close. To put an unspoken stamp on her that read *mine*. He'd learned over the years how to throw up a protective wall on the rare instance he needed privacy, a subtle signal for others to keep their distance. Most recognized and obeyed, and this occasion proved no different.

Of course it helped that his staff ran interference whenever he gave them that certain look. Footmen shifted their positions. Matrons were intercepted and their hopeful daughters distracted by accommodating friends. It all occurred with the beauty and timing of an intricate dance with no one, he hoped, the wiser—especially not the woman on his arm.

A clear path opened to the buffet set up in an anteroom adjacent to the ballroom, and Lander headed in that direction. Helping himself to one of the fragile china plates embossed with the Montgomery family crest, he filled it with a selection of tidbits. He dipped a strawberry in the molten chocolate fountain and offered it to her. To his amusement, she bit into the strawberry, her eyes half closing as she savored the rich dark chocolate.

"Come on. I know someplace private we can go to eat this."

Bypassing the scattering of linen-covered tables, Lander led Juliana through the open French doors to the gardens beyond. Subtle lighting glowed along the gravel walkways and in the trees and shrubbery. He hooked a sharp right onto a path that most overlooked.

"You know your way around," she observed.

"I've been here once or twice before."

The path dead-ended at a small lattice-covered gazebo. Vines twined up the posts and across the top, dripping fat white rose blossoms. Their fragrant scent hung heavily in the air, ripe and eager to lend assistance to a scene set for seduction.

Lander plucked one of the plumpest roses, and after thumbing off the thorns, threaded it behind her ear. He allowed the back of his hand to trail along her cheek and down the endless length of her neck. He was amazed at the softness of her skin, the color and texture putting the rose to shame. Even the scent of her rivaled the most potent flower.

"How did you come to be here?" he demanded.

"Does it matter?"

"No. Right now it doesn't matter in the least. Only one thing does."

He tossed aside the plate he carried. Neither of them were hungry, at least not for food. Sliding his hands up along the bare length of her arms, he dipped his fingers into the heavy mass of auburn curls and tugged her close. She came willingly, lifting her face to his.

Night shadows turned her eyes black, the moonlight picking out the occasional glitter of gold that slipped past the darkness. Her heart thudded against his, tripping light and eager. A soft smile tilted her mouth and he wondered if her lips were as soft as her skin.

His younger brother, Merrick, had been labeled the impulsive one in the family practically from the moment of his birth, with his stepsister, Miri, close but not quite as bad. Lander had always chosen a more disciplined route. Steady. In charge. He allowed little to sway or influence him.

But he had only to look at Juliana to want with a ferocity beyond his control. He didn't care that the Verdonian election to choose whether or not he'd be the next king was only months away. He didn't care that the press had him beneath a microscope. He didn't even care that in all likelihood the woman he held within his arms wouldn't make an appropriate wife, let alone an appropriate queen. All that mattered was finding a way to carry her off to his bed and lose himself in the fiery heat of her.

Taking his time, he lowered his head and captured her mouth. Lightly. Just a gentle sample. Just enough to test flavor and texture. But that was all it took. One taste and he was lost. His mouth returned to hers and her hands curled into his shirt, anchoring him in place. Not that he planned on going anywhere.

The kiss seemed to change with each and every breath. First fast and impatient, two people discovering a new, irresistible sweet—and desperate to sate their craving of it. Then curious, each eager to explore every detail about the other. Next came slow and languid as they savored what they'd discovered, relishing the ability to please, before the want grew too strong, the urgency too powerful to deny. The kiss turned stormy again. Demanding. Pulsing. Hard and reckless. Robbing them of all thought. He heard her moan and inhaled the sound, reveling in the helpless sign of desire.

With each passing minute, with every hungry, biting kiss, his need for her coalesced into one inescapable certainty. Once she found out who he really was, there would be hell to pay. But he didn't care. It would be worth it. Because no matter what obstacles he had to overcome, no matter who stood in his way, this woman was his and he intended to have her.

Two

She was lost. Totally lost.

Juliana opened her mouth to his and drank greedily, aware that if there had been a bed here in the middle of their private glade, she'd have been on her back, opening herself to this man, giving herself to someone she'd known less than an hour. The knowledge had her shuddering in a combination of disbelief and desire.

His hands drifted from her hair to her shoulders before skating down the naked length of her spine. He cupped her hips, tugging her against him until she was locked tight against his pelvis. She struggled to think, to speak, to plead. But even that was beyond her. All she could do was moan her encouragement. His hands were large and hard and she wanted them on her, wanted them to touch her in the most intimate ways possible, just as she wanted to touch him.

Impatient, she snagged his bow tie and ripped it from its mooring. The pearl studs holding his shirt closed scattered beneath her urgent fingers. And then finally, *finally,* she hit hot, masculine flesh. She ran her hands across his chest and downward over hard, rippled abs.

He returned the favor, finding the crystal button at the nape of her neck and slipping it through its hole. The cap sleeves of her gown slid down her arms and he eased back, tracing the swell of her breasts above the corsetted bodice. Gently he slid the silk downward, baring her. They both stood motionless for a long moment. The only sound was the desperate harshness of their breathing. Moonlight silvered them, giving ripe flesh an unearthly glow. The scent of roses mingled with that of desire.

"God, you're beautiful," he murmured.

"I want you. As crazy as that sounds, I do." She laughed unevenly. "Maybe it's something in the air."

"Or maybe we were meant to be here, like this."

"Fate?"

He shrugged. "It's as good a reason as any."

As though unable to resist, he reached for her, tracing his fingertip down the swell of her breast to her nipple. His face remained taut and hungry, filled with a determination she found impossible to resist.

It took two attempts before she could speak. "I don't even know your name." That simple fact both bewildered and excited.

"We know this." His hand cupped her breast and he leaned down to feather a kiss across the tip, eliciting another helpless moan. "This is all that matters."

She hovered between common sense and lust. She craved this man, craved his touch, his kisses, his body.

It didn't matter that she'd only met him a scant hour ago. It had only taken one look, one single touch, for her to be willing to compromise the values and mores she held most dear.

She'd never done anything like this before nor wanted a man quite so desperately. Even with Stewart, with the man who'd ultimately betrayed her, she'd never come close to experiencing such a total rending of control. If she'd learned nothing else from her past, it had been to live with the utmost caution. To keep rampant emotions in tight check. As a result, she'd turned logic and rationale into her own personal religion. And yet, here she stood, ready to dive headfirst into a fast-moving river leading straight over a waterfall. Not that she cared. This one man, along with this one moment in time, governed every thought and deed.

"We can't do anything here," she felt compelled to protest. "Someone might find us."

"In that case we have two options. We can stop. Or we can take this somewhere else." He made the suggestion without inflection. And though he continued to hold her, he didn't use those clever hands to try and influence her decision. "It's up to you."

He was offering her a clear-cut choice, an opportunity to back out while there was still time. But she'd already made that choice. There was only one option available to her. She lifted her arms and wrapped them around his neck. Finding his mouth with hers, she sank into the kiss, offering herself without saying a word. It was glorious. Delicious. A fantasy beyond compare. If this were a dream, she hoped never to awake. His arms offered a world she'd never known, but one that she wanted more than anything. A world of passion and seduction, and oddly enough, protection. If she were very lucky, this night would never end.

She snatched a final kiss before pulling back. "I'd like to go somewhere else," she said answering his question. The ease and simplicity of her response amazed her. How right it felt and how deliriously free she felt saying it. "I'd like to go with you very much."

With an exclamation of triumph, he swept her into his arms. She grinned up at him about to demand that he carry her off to his fairy-tale castle and have his wicked way with her, when the sound of someone clearing his throat came from the edge of the copse. Instantly her "prince" spun them around into shadow, putting his back to whomever had joined them. He lowered her to the ground, refastening her gown to conceal her nudity.

"Bad timing, Lander?" a laughing voice asked.

"Damn it, Joc. Two minutes more and we'd have been gone."

Juliana stiffened. No. Oh, please no. It couldn't be. A single, swift glance confirmed her worst fears. She gave herself a few precious seconds to catch her breath while mustering what little poise she still retained. Circling the man Joc had referred to as Lander—and why did that name send a warning bell screaming though her fogged brain?—she stepped into a patch of moonlight.

"Hello, Joc," she greeted her brother.

"Juliana?" He uttered her name in sharp disbelief.

Lander's gaze switched from one to the other, his eyes narrowing. "You two know each other?"

"I work for Arnaud's Angels," she responded calmly, shooting her brother a look, warning that she didn't want him to reveal their relationship. To her relief, he gave a subtle nod of understanding. "I didn't realize Mr. Arnaud would be here tonight."

"No," Joc murmured dryly. "Obviously, you didn't."

"If you'll excuse me…Lander, is it?" She knew that name. How did she know that name? If only she could think straight. "I'll leave you two gentlemen to your business."

Joc lifted an eyebrow. "Don't be rude, my dear. As a representative of Arnaud's Angels you owe His Highness more respect than that. After all, he is your host."

Lander started to speak, but after making a sound of disgust, fell silent.

Juliana stilled. "What are you talking about?" But deep down, she knew. His name had sounded familiar, and perhaps if she hadn't been so drunk on kisses she'd have recognized it sooner.

Joc released a bark of disbelieving laughter. "Didn't you realize? The man you've been kissing is Prince Lander. Or to be more precise, Prince Lander Montgomery, Duke of Verdon. The Lion of Mt. Roche."

Oh, no. It couldn't be. What wicked-humored fate had put her in the path of the one man she wanted most to avoid? And why hadn't she figured it out sooner? How was it possible that the very first time she'd chosen to cut loose, she'd selected to do it with him? When it came to ignorant fools, she took top prize in both categories. Lifting her chin, she faced Prince Lander with what little remained of her tattered dignity.

"How very amusing," she said, her tone making it clear she was anything but amused. She swept him a deep, formal curtsey. "I'm delighted I could provide Your Highness with tonight's entertainment."

"It wasn't like that and you damn well know it."

She could hear the frustration underscoring his words, but didn't care. He'd kept his identity from her for reasons of his own, even after she'd made it clear that she had no interest in meeting Prince Lander. Maybe he'd remained silent because she'd warned him that she'd run if she came across anyone of consequence. Otherwise, he'd have revealed his name if only in the hope that it would have her tumbling into his bed all that more quickly.

More quickly? She almost groaned aloud. How much faster could she have tumbled? It had only taken him a brief hour to sweep her off her feet, and that was without pulling rank, as it were. Murmuring an excuse, she skirted her brother and returned to the palace. She hesitated in the shadows just beyond the spill of lights from the ballroom, struggling to regain her self-control.

How could she have been so idiotic? How could she have let a man—even a prince—rob her of every ounce of intelligent thought? But from the moment she'd first seen him, she'd been utterly lost, willing to go anywhere he demanded, give anything he requested, do whatever he required. The knowledge ate at her. With one painful exception, she'd never allowed a man so much control over her. And yet in the space of a single hour, Prince Lander had not only demanded that control, but had been given it without a single word of protest. Had she learned nothing from her past? Clearly not.

Taking a deep breath, she stepped into the light and headed across the ballroom, walking casually, if determinedly, toward the nearest exit. Before she'd taken more than a half-dozen steps, a hand landed on her shoulder, spinning her around.

"I'm sure you don't intend to leave without dancing with me," Joc stated. Not giving her a chance to protest,

he swung her onto the dance floor. "So, tell me…
What's a nice girl like you doing in a palace like this?"

"Oh, ha-ha. The more interesting question is, what are
you doing here?" Juliana retorted in a furious undertone.

"Visiting you, of course."

Blithe and casual. Typical of him. But she wasn't
buying it for a minute. She knew that beneath that
good-ol'-boy routine hid the soul of a brilliant, hard-
as-nails businessman. Whatever reason Joc had for
being here, it was neither blithe nor casual. "You
came all the way to Verdonia just to visit me? Try
again, big brother."

"Maybe I should ask what you're doing with
Prince Lander."

As usual, he'd turned the tables on her with annoying
ease. She focused on the dance for a full minute before
replying. "I didn't know he was a prince."

"Or you'd never have been with him?"

She hated the gentle concern in Joc's voice almost
as much as she hated the question. "Not a chance."

His breath escaped in a sigh. "Just as well. I wouldn't
want any sister of mine mixed up with a Montgomery."

Her head jerked up at that. "Why not?"

"We have a…history."

"What sort of history?" she pressed.

"That's not important."

Impatience lined Joc's face, warning her to drop
the subject. It was a striking face, lean and golden, with
the blood of their Comanche ancestors contributing to
the impressive bone structure. Black eyes, black hair
and what some would call a black heart completed the
package, though she knew better. Joc was the kindest,
most generous man alive. Unless crossed.

"Explain something to me, Ana—"

"Juliana," she corrected. "I don't use my nickname, anymore."

"And why is that?" he demanded. "Why don't you want him to know who you are? What does it matter if I tell him you're Juliana Rose Arnaud, my sister, rather than Juliana Rose, charity worker? You won't be seeing him again." He waited a beat before pushing. "Will you?"

"No." But how she wanted to.

Deep grooves formed on either side of his mouth. "It's because you're my sister, isn't it? That's why you only use your first and middle names these days. Because you're afraid of the attention you'll receive if anyone finds out you're Ana Arnaud, sister to the infamous Joc Arnaud."

Tears filled her eyes and she blinked them back before lifting her gaze to his, praying that he wouldn't be able to tell how close to the edge he'd pushed her. She lifted a hand to his cheek. "It's not that. You know I love you. I'm proud to be your sister."

"Then what stopped you from telling Montgomery the truth?"

She shivered at the coldness of the question…and the underlying hurt. "I haven't told anyone. I want the focus to be on the charity, not on me. Now that I know Lander is a prince, it's even more imperative that I remain silent. He's in the public eye. If the media gets a whiff of our involvement, they'll be all over us. I can't handle that. Not again." Not ever again. "Don't you see? It's not just what will happen to me. It's not fair to throw Prince Lander to the wolves without any warning."

"Is that the only reason? Because if it is, I can take care of the media."

The hard look in Joc's eyes worried her. There was

another reason she couldn't be with Prince Lander, but she didn't dare mention it. It would only anger her brother. "I came to Verdonia to escape scandal, not stir up more. Besides, it isn't like I'm seriously interested in Prince Lander."

"Liar." He hesitated, no doubt torn between whatever history stood between the two men and his love for her. "I may not care much for your choice, but if you're serious about him, I can fix things," he offered grudgingly. "Though to be honest, I'd rather you kept your distance. I don't trust the man. Not with you."

"What you saw in the garden, it was just a bit of harmless fun. Nothing consequential. And it's not like I'll be in Verdonia for very much longer. A few more weeks at most." Could Joc hear the desperation in her voice? Probably. Her brother was as skilled at reading people as he was at making money. In fact, she doubted he'd have amassed his current fortune if he hadn't possessed both abilities. "Tomorrow I'll be back at work and tonight will have been nothing more than a sweet dream. Just a meaningless interlude."

"And Montgomery?"

She took a deep breath. "Since you don't want me to see him again, I won't be seeing him." For some reason the realization caused a stab of pain.

"Montgomery's a powerful man. If he wants you, he'll find you."

She shook her head. "He won't waste time trying. After all, it was only one dance."

"And one kiss," Joc added. "No big deal."

She flinched. "Exactly." She deliberately changed the subject. "I guess I have you to thank for the ticket to the ball, as well as the dress."

"Considering how hard you've been working, you deserve it," he answered, accepting the new topic with good grace. "It only seemed appropriate to send a suitable dress and shoes. I'm willing to bet you didn't bring anything with you."

"Good guess. Maybe that's because I'm here to work, not play."

"Speaking of which, the reports I've received have been glowing."

"Thank you." His acknowledgment of her accomplishments delighted her. Although Joc wasn't stingy with his praise, he also didn't offer it gratuitously. "And thank you for tonight. It's been—" Amazing. Incredible. A dream come true. "Very nice."

He leaned forward and kissed her brow. "You're welcome. I don't suppose you're ready to come home now?"

"Home?" It took her a minute to catch his drift. "Oh, you mean to the States?"

"Of course I mean to the States." Amusement competed with impatience. "Honey, as wonderful a job as you're doing here, I need you back in Dallas. You're my best executive accountant."

"Was," she stressed. "I *was* your best executive accountant. Now I head up your European branch of Arnaud's Angels."

He waved that aside. "A total waste of your talent."

Her mouth tightened. "I don't happen to agree. The children need me."

"You mean…you need the children."

Sometimes it didn't pay to be subtle with her brother. "I'm not returning to Dallas."

"It doesn't have to be Dallas, if you'd rather not."

His instant willingness to compromise warned of his seriousness. "You can work out of whichever city suits you."

"What suits me is the job I'm currently doing. Considering how much work there is for me in Europe, I may never return home." Her hand tightened on his shoulder. "I need you to back off, Joc, and let me live my life my way. Either I continue with Angels or I offer my services to some other charitable organization. I guarantee they'll snatch me up in a heartbeat."

To her surprise, he let it go. "Fine, fine. If that's what you want, stay in Verdonia. Hell, stay wherever in Europe you want." A frown touched his brow. "So long as it's away from Montgomery, I can live with it."

Lander stood on the sidelines, watching Joc and Juliana dance with an ease that spoke of long intimacy. Damn it all! It might have been a replay of their years at Harvard. For some reason, they'd constantly found themselves in competition. On the playing field. In the classroom. And in their most contentious battles, over women. After the first few years where they'd taken loutish delight in poaching, their attitudes had changed. Lander hadn't wanted any of the women Arnaud had been with, anymore than Joc had wanted Lander's.

But that changed the moment Lander had met Juliana. Now only one question remained…was Juliana fair game? And what did he do if she wasn't?

The dance ended. But Joc didn't release his hold on his partner. Rather, they spoke quietly for a moment before he bent forward and gave her a second kiss, this one on the cheek. It took every ounce of self-control for

Lander to keep his shoulder glued to the wall instead of striding across the room and planting his fist in Arnaud's nose. If that kiss had landed any closer to Juliana's mouth he might have, regardless of the consequences.

The couple reluctantly parted—at least, it appeared reluctant to Lander—and the crowd chose that inopportune moment to surge forward, blocking his view. When next he could see, only Joc remained, who offered a nod of acknowledgment and headed toward Lander, joining him on the sidelines.

"I think it's time we spoke, don't you?" Joc asked.

Screw that. "Where is she?"

"Gone."

"Is she yours?" Lander demanded with single-minded intensity.

Anger flared in Joc's gaze. "That's a hell of a thing to ask. Juliana doesn't belong to any man. Not me. And for damn sure not you. Not now. Not ever."

Not ever? He'd see about that. "If she's not yours, I want to know where I can reach her."

"Did you hear what I said?"

"I heard. Are you telling me she's off-limits?"

A silent battle of wills ensued with Joc blinking first. "Is she that important to you?"

"Yes."

Joc shrugged his concession, but Lander could see the wheels turning. Ever the businessman, he was no doubt trying to figure out how to turn the situation to his financial advantage. "Fine. But don't you have more important issues to deal with than some woman you only met tonight? Isn't that why you called me?"

It shouldn't have taken Lander a full minute to switch his focus from Juliana to affairs of state. But it did. Aw, hell. He scrubbed a hand across his face. He had it bad. Without another word, Lander led the way to his private office. It was a large room with floor-to-ceiling windows that offered an unparalleled view of each day's sunrise. The room also overlooked the front of the palace, and Lander made a point of crossing to the window just in time to see a distinctive flash of silver silk disappear into the back of a cab.

Deliberately forcing himself to redirect his focus to the current problems plaguing his country, he turned to face Joc Arnaud. His nemesis stood in front of a map of Verdonia, his hands clasped behind his back.

"So when will you be crowned king?"

"Either in two months—" Lander shrugged "—or never."

"Never?" Joc swiveled, his brows climbing. "I don't understand. Wasn't your father king? I assumed when he died that the crown would fall to you. Isn't that how those things work?"

Lander inclined his head. "In a true monarchy that would be correct. But in Verdonia it's a little different. We have a popular vote among the eligible royals."

Joc frowned. "You and your brother have to compete for the throne?"

"As a second son Merrick's not in the running. No, the eldest royals from each principality are the only ones eligible."

"Well, hell. Who are you up against?" Joc leaned in and tapped the southernmost principality. "I gather you represent Verdon."

Lander joined Arnaud in front of the map and indicated the principality farthest north. "Prince Brandt von Folke is the eligible royal from Avernos."

Joc traced the principality snuggled between north and south. "And this one in the middle? Celestia, is it?"

"There aren't any eligible royals. You have to be twenty-five to rule Verdonia and Princess Alyssa won't turn twenty-five until after the election. She's my brother, Merrick's, wife. They married just a few days ago."

"A political affair?"

Lander nodded. "It started out that way. She was going to marry Brandt until Merrick intervened."

"Why would Merrick inter—" Joc broke off, his brow furrowed. "Oh, I get it. If Alyssa and this Brandt fellow had married, it would have united the royal families of Avernos and Celestia. Wouldn't that have ensured Prince Brandt the popular vote?"

"Astute as always," Lander commented. Joc's talent at grasping the salient points and analyzing how they affected the big picture had always—reluctantly—impressed the hell out of him. "Yes, Brandt would have won the election if Merrick hadn't interfered. He abducted Alyssa and married her himself."

Joc barked out an incredulous laugh. "Gutsy."

"Would have been if he hadn't fallen in love with her."

"I don't know." Joc's expression turned dubious. "You certain he wasn't ensuring you the win by uniting the Montgomerys with her people? Sounds damn convenient if you ask me."

Lander fought back a stab of anger. "I think he'd have claimed it was quite inconvenient. But if you saw them together—" he shrugged "—they appear disgustingly happy."

Joc glanced across the room and brightened. Crossing to Lander's desk, he helped himself to a Havana Corona from the humidor. "Okay, so now that you've caught me up on the political situation, why don't you explain what I'm doing here." Making himself at home, he clipped the cigar and passed it to Lander before repeating the process for himself. "I gather there's a serious reason or you wouldn't have imposed on our...friendship."

Lander didn't bother couching his words. "I need your help." He took his time lighting his cigar, before lifting his gaze to stare at Arnaud through the haze of pungent smoke. "Verdonia's in trouble."

"I assume you mean financial difficulties. I suppose you expect me to bail you out just because I owe you over a half-forgotten college debt?"

"If it were half-forgotten, you wouldn't be here." He allowed his comment to hang, before adding, "And I'll only accept your help if you can do it aboveboard."

Joc bit down on his cigar, fury burning in his gaze. "You have a hell of a nerve." A hint of rawness ripped through his voice. "My father may have walked the wrong side of the line. At least, that's what the feds claimed. And he may have fathered a pair of bastard children on my mother and then refused to give them his name. But I'm not, and never have been, my father. I only deal aboveboard and if you've had me investigated, as I'm sure you have, you damn well know that."

Lander inclined his head. "That's the only reason we're talking. Tell me something, Arnaud. How many failing businesses have you turned around?"

"Too many to count."

"Right now Verdonia is a failing business. I need your skill—and maybe a few Arnaud business interests relocating here—to get my country turned around."

Joc worked on his cigar before slowly nodding. "If

there's money to be made helping, I'll help. But I'll want an airtight contract before I let go of one thin dime."

"Perfect. First we'll talk money." Lander opened a decanter and splashed a couple fingers of single malt into a crystal tumbler. He held it out. "And then we'll talk women."

Three

Juliana cuddled Harver in her arms as she spoke quietly to the baby's mother. Born with a cleft palate, the little boy would be another of Arnaud's Angels. At least, he would if Juliana had her way. She had doctors standing by once she received approval from Harver's parents for the operation.

The mother was understandably fearful, while the father appeared suspicious of the offer of such an expensive procedure for free, despite her having explained everything with meticulous care. It helped that the surgeon was Verdonian, his calm voice of reason allaying most concerns. At long last the parents signed the consent forms and Harver was carried off for the necessary testing in preparation for his surgery.

After wishing the parents well, and receiving a fierce hug from Harver's mother, Juliana gathered up her paperwork and filed the various forms and folders in her briefcase. As always, an irrepressible excitement bubbled through her now that her task was completed, now that she knew another baby would receive the life-altering procedure. How could Joc think an accounting job, no matter how lofty the position, could compare to this?

She exited the hospital, her high spirits giving a swing to her step as she headed toward a nearby cab stand. A light breeze tugged at her hair, loosening a few of the curls that she'd secured at the nape of her neck with a clip. She hadn't gone more than a dozen paces when a black stretch limo pulled up beside her. She sensed who it was even before the door swung open to reveal Prince Lander.

Dismay filled her. So he'd found her. She shouldn't be surprised. It was bound to happen. Her grip tightened on her briefcase as she inclined her head. "Your Highness."

"Please, get in, Ms. Rose," he said. "We need to talk."

Just because he was a prince didn't mean she had to go with him. She'd made enough of a fool of herself the previous evening without making it worse in the harsh light of day. "No, thank you. I think we said everything we needed to last night."

"Perhaps." He paused a telling moment. "But we didn't do everything we planned, did we?"

She fought to control the flush that heated her cheeks. "Fortunately. Now if you'll excuse me—"

"I'm not going anywhere. And neither are you." Determination settled into the hard lines of his face. She recognized that expression. She should. Joc wore it often enough and it always signaled an unwillingness to budge from his position. "Now are you going to get in, or do I continue to draw attention to us by following you?"

He couldn't have found a more effective way of convincing her to join him. Caving to the inevitable, she slid in beside him, placing her briefcase between them. Let him read whatever he wished into that small, pointless gesture.

"Okay, speak." She closed her eyes, drawing on every ounce of self-control. "Please excuse me, Your Highness. I apologize if that sounded rude. How can Arnaud's Angels be of assistance to you?"

"I'm not interested in your charitable work," he bit out. "I'm interested in you, as you damn well know."

"Yes, sir. I believe you explained that last night. Perhaps we didn't have an opportunity to finish that conversation, after all. So allow me to finish it now."

She forced herself to turn and offer her coldest stare. It was a major mistake. She'd mapped out precisely what she'd intended to say, worked it almost like a mathematical equation—the words, the intonation, the expression she'd use. But in the space of the two heartbeats it took for her to fall into his intense gaze, every last thought vanished from her head. She could only stare at him in complete and utter bewilderment.

"Fine," he prompted. "Finish it."

"Finish it." She moistened her lips. "Right. I'll do that right now."

Held by those brilliant hazel eyes, she racked her brain, struggling to remember what she was supposed to finish. Something. Something about…finishing. Her confusion must have shown because his mouth twitched. And then a chuckle rumbled deep in his chest. "Hell, woman. We do have a bizarre effect on each other, don't we?"

She couldn't help it; his laughter proved too contagious. Shaking her head, she gave in to her amusement. "What am I going to do about you, Your Highness?"

"Whatever you want. And make it Lander."

"Thank you." She regarded him with sudden suspicion. "How did you find me? Joc?"

"No. He refused to help."

She could be grateful for that much, at least. For some reason their shared amusement had her relaxing enough for her brain to function again. "I remember what I was going to say."

"Something about finishing?" he offered with a slight smile.

She nodded gravely. "Finishing things between us."

"Excellent. I'll instruct my driver to drop us off at the palace so we can finish what we started last night."

She fought to keep from laughing again. She didn't want to be charmed by him. Yet she was. Utterly charmed. Enthralled. Entertained. Filled with an impossible yearning. It had to stop, and stop now. "I meant finishing, as in ending things between us," she clarified.

"Why?"

The simple question caught her off guard. "Last night… It wasn't meant to happen."

"But it did. You wanted me. You can't deny that."

Honesty came hard, but she refused to shy from it. "I don't deny it. I wish I could blame it on the moonlight. Or on too much to drink."

"It wasn't even close to a full moon. And you didn't have anything alcoholic."

"No, I didn't." If only she had, it would be some balm to her pride. "I take full responsibility for what happened."

"Noble, but unnecessary." Irony laced his words. "I seem to recall you weren't alone in that garden."

"But I let you—" She'd let him kiss her. Incredible, amazing kisses. And he'd touched her. Just remembering had her aching to have his hands on her again.

He studied her, pinning her with a look that had her brain misfiring again. "Are you feeling guilty because of Joc?"

She blinked in bewilderment. "Joc? What does he have to do with this?"

"He asked for two invitations when I invited him to the ball. I assume he sent the second to you. And I'm also guessing he might have had something to do with your designer gown, as well. Didn't you tell me it was a gift?"

He didn't know. Relief swept through her. He'd assumed she and Joc were lovers. Her brother had promised he wouldn't tell Lander of their connection, but she'd been concerned that the prince might have guessed the truth. She nodded. "Joc arranged for both the clothes and the invitation."

"Is that why you want to end things between us? Are the two of you involved?"

"Not the way you mean."

His eyes narrowed in thought. "In that case, there can only be one other reason. It's because of who I am, isn't it?"

She couldn't hold his gaze. "Yes."

"Hell." She could hear the ripe frustration vented in that single expletive. "You're probably the first woman I've ever met who didn't want to have anything to do with me once she knew who I was."

"Takes all kinds," she joked.

"Explain it to me."

She forced herself to look at him, to be as honest as possible. He deserved no less. "I don't like living in the spotlight. Being with you, even for a short time, would mean precisely that."

"Been there, done that?"

"Yes."

"With Joc."

He didn't phrase it as a question or ask for a confirmation, so she didn't offer one. Instead, she reached for the door. "May I go now, Your Highness?"

He gave an impatient shake of his head. "I'll take you home." Before she could protest, he signaled his driver. "Samson Apartments," he instructed.

"How do you know where I live?" When he simply smiled, she released her breath in a sigh. "Why do I bother asking? You're Prince Lander, Duke of Verdon. I suppose all you have to do is wave your royal scepter and your every command is granted."

"If that were true, we wouldn't be having this conversation. We'd both be in my suite at the palace and you'd be gracing my bed."

There was nothing she could say to that, so she closed her mouth and turned her head to stare out the window. The drive through the city was accomplished at a record pace, and in short order they pulled up outside her apartment complex.

"I guess this is goodbye," she said, reaching for the door handle.

"It is." He paused a beat. "If that's what you really want."

"We settled this already."

"You can leave." He shifted closer and covered her hand with his, preventing her escape. His breath stirred the curls at her temple while his voice murmured seductively in her ear. "You can get out and we'll never see each other again. Or you can stay. Think about it. We can have one evening together before we go our separate ways. No one has to know. I can arrange that. No media attention. No spotlight. Just a man and a woman doing what men and women have done throughout the ages. One night, Juliana."

One night. The insidious words were all too tempting. She could see it, as clearly as though it had already happened. A night she'd never forget, held within the arms of a man who filled her with a desire beyond anything she'd ever before experienced. Limbs intertwined. Heated flesh sliding against heated flesh. An intimate exploration as soft and gentle as it was hard and fierce. She'd never allowed herself to give in to such basic, primitive demands. For the first time, she wanted to.

"Don't," she whispered.

"Because you're not interested in what I'm offering?"

She shook her head. "Because I am."

He tucked a lock of hair behind her ear, his mouth following the same path as his fingers. "Then why resist?"

She fought back a moan. It was an excellent question. Why did she resist? She was far from home. No one knew her true identity. Nor did anyone know about the various scandals in her past. Hadn't she been cautious her entire life, watching every step she took? And even that hadn't prevented her from tripping. Now she had an opportunity that would never come her way again. A chance to seize what she wanted. Have the sort of fling she'd never dared indulge in before—never been tempted to indulge in.

"If I come with you," she began hesitantly, "what would you expect from me? Where would we go?"

"I expect nothing more than what you're willing to give. And we can go anyplace you'd like."

He interlaced her fingers with his and lifted them from the door handle. She allowed it, realizing as she did so that she'd just committed herself to insanity. She didn't know whether to laugh at her daring or call herself every sort of fool. Perhaps both.

"Can we go somewhere other than the palace?" she asked.

He inclined his head in agreement. "Someplace private."

"You're actually allowed privacy?"

"Allowed? No. But every once in a while I take what I need." His smile came slow and deliberate. "And right now what I need is you. Give me a moment to arrange everything."

The entire time he was gone she sat in utter disbelief. What had she done? How could she have agreed to see him again when she knew the potential consequences? Last night she could blame on moonlight and roses, on wanting so desperately to believe in fairy tales that she'd behaved in ways she never would have believed herself capable. Now, with a clear, bright June sun shining down on her, she couldn't delude herself any longer. The facts were as black-and-white as a column of numbers. It didn't matter how many times she totaled the figures, the bottom line didn't change. And the bottom line right now was she'd just agreed to spend the night with Lander.

Her mouth firmed. So what if she had? Why shouldn't she indulge in a single night of bliss before returning to real life? It wasn't that she deserved it, or had earned it. She simply wanted it. Wanted the fantasy. Wanted the intense pleasure she'd shared with Lander to continue a short time longer. She slid her hand over the plush leather seat. For once she'd be greedy. She'd put aside all her fears and worries and grab with both hands what fate had so generously provided. As for tomorrow?

She lifted her chin in defiance. Tomorrow could take care of itself.

A few minutes later Lander returned to the limo. "Everything all right?" he asked.

"Perfect."

"I was hesitant to leave you alone in case you had second thoughts."

"Oh, I had second thoughts. And third and fourth and fifth."

"You're still here."

She offered a blinding smile. "Yes, I am."

He cupped her chin in response. Lifting her face, he took her mouth in a slow, deliberate kiss. She was curious to see what would happen, whether she'd react to him the same way as before. To her dismay she found it far different.

Last night she'd been lost. Totally and utterly lost. It had been like discovering a glorious private world, filled with beauty of sound and taste, scent and sensation. She'd been intrigued by what she'd discovered, but able to explore only the smallest part. Last night she'd barely stepped into that world.

Today it exploded around her, everything twice as intense, twice as spectacular, twice as overwhelming. And it left her utterly bewildered. A kiss was supposed to be just a kiss. A sweet joining of lips. A mild physical pleasure. Not this blistering desire that melted all intelligent thought. That had never happened to her before.

Lander reluctantly released her. "We're in serious trouble. You realize that, don't you?"

"We can handle it," she insisted. Did he catch the hint of desperation in her voice? "One night. That's all we can have. After that, we go our separate ways."

"Hell, woman. We can barely handle a simple kiss. You think after I make love to you, we'll be able to walk away from each other?"

"You promised!"

A hint of anger glinted in his eyes. "I've never broken my word, and I don't intend to start now, no matter how much I'd like to."

She'd have to be satisfied with that. "Where are we going?" she asked, intent on changing the subject.

"I have access to an apartment on the outskirts of the city. It's a secure location. With luck, no one will discover we're there."

To her relief, he was right. The limo pulled into a deserted underground garage and dropped them off by a private elevator before departing again. In less than two minutes the elevator whisked them upward, opening onto a penthouse suite. Lander locked the elevator in place to ensure they didn't receive any surprise visitors, before joining her in the middle of the foyer.

"It's lovely," Juliana murmured, struggling to conceal the distressing awkwardness sweeping through her.

"Feel free to look around."

Taking him at his word, she wandered from the foyer into a great room walled on two sides with windows overlooking the city of Mt. Roche. Adjacent to that she found a formal dining room with a compact kitchen beyond. Lander didn't follow her. Instead, he took up a stance between the foyer and great room, his gaze on her the entire time. Returning to her starting point she glanced toward the one section of the apartment she hadn't yet explored.

"Don't," Lander said.

She looked at him, startled. "Don't what?"

"It's the bedroom. You're welcome to check it out." He tilted his head to one side. "But somehow I don't think you're ready for that."

She wrapped her arms about her waist. "Is it so obvious?"

"What's obvious is that you're not ready for any of this." He straightened from his stance and approached. "If I were less selfish, I'd take you home. But I can't. I want you too much. And I think you want me, too."

As nervous as she was, she couldn't deny the truth. "You know I do."

"If you were willing to give me more than one night, we could avoid tonight's dilemma. We'd have the time to take our relationship slow and easy. What do you say? Wouldn't a gradual progression suit you far more than fast and reckless?" Wordless, she shook her head and he accepted her refusal with a shrug. "In that case, will you stay, or should we end this now?"

She hesitated. How could she have thought herself capable of a one-night stand with him? To go into it so cold-bloodedly when she'd never indulged in one before. She glanced uneasily across the foyer. If Lander hadn't locked the elevator, she'd be over there right now, stabbing at the button, determined to escape. She needed an out, even just the promise of one, so she wouldn't feel quite so much like a mouse caught beneath a cat's paw.

She cleared her voice. "If this doesn't work—"

"I'll take you home." Amusement rippled through his

words and she realized he'd been able to read her thoughts as though she'd shouted them aloud. "In the meantime, no pressure. I'll open a bottle of wine and we can talk."

"Sounds perfect."

And it was. They decided to watch the sunset from the balcony off the great room. Lander chose a French Beaujolais that went down as smooth and light as the conversation. He asked about her work with Arnaud's Angels, a subject dear to her heart. As they talked and drank, Juliana could feel her tension ease. They finished their wine just as the sun vanished behind the Mt. Roche skyline. The city lights sparkled in the growing darkness, winking up at the stars dotting the velvet canopy overhead.

Lander rose, offering his hand. "Are you hungry? I arranged for dinner to be delivered. It won't take long to heat."

She gazed up at him, wishing with all her heart that Lander were an ordinary man, or that she didn't have a past that curtailed any possibility of a relationship. That she were the sort of woman he could be seen with in public. Or he was in a position not to care about propriety or scandal.

Taking his hand, she stood. "Thank you, I'm starved. I worked through lunch today."

He maintained his stance, his face cast into shadow, while hers was bared by the light seeping onto the balcony from the great room. "What were you thinking about a minute ago?" he asked unexpectedly.

She regarded him warily. "Nothing important."

"Did you know that your eyes darken when you're not being honest?" He cupped her face, sweeping his thumbs along her cheekbones. "The brown swallows up the gold. Tell me the truth. What were you thinking?"

"That I was sorry we don't have longer than tonight," she confessed.

"That's your choice, not mine."

"Trust me when I say I have a valid reason."

"Tell me what it is."

"Maybe after dinner." He shook his head, rejecting the possibility, and she sighed. "My eyes, again?"

"Dead giveaway."

"Joc could always tell when I was lying, too. Now I know why."

She'd made a mistake mentioning her brother, she realized. Lander's hazel eyes didn't darken as hers had. Instead they flamed with odd green sparks. He shifted closer, joining her inside the circle of light. It sliced across his face, revealing the fierceness of his expression.

"I think it might be wise to leave your boss out of our conversation tonight." His voice scored the balmy dark with a wintry coldness. "Unless you want this night to end far differently than planned."

She considered backing down. But it had never been her style. She might be unwilling to reveal her true relationship with Joc or confess to the various scandals in her background. That didn't mean she'd allow him to believe she was one of her brother's women. "Are you jealous? Is that why you don't want me to mention Joc?"

"Yes."

He'd surprised her with his honesty. "Then allow me to reassure you. He and I aren't lovers. Not now. Not ever."

"Your relationship is strictly professional?" Lander asked dubiously.

"No," she admitted. "It's more than that, and always will be. We've known each other most our lives."

"Let me guess. He's like a brother to you."

She couldn't help but smile. "Exactly."

"I find it impossible to believe there's a man alive who could be around you for any length of time and not want you in his bed. Especially a man like Joc."

"Look at my eyes and tell me what you see. Truth... or lie?"

He took his time, his hands continuing to skim across her face as if he could absorb the information through his fingertips. After an endless minute his mouth curved to one side. "Truth."

"Is there anything else you want to ask me about Joc? Now's your chance."

"Not a thing."

"Good." She grinned. "In that case, let's eat. I really am starving."

She helped him heat their dinner and carry the meals to the table. "My stepmother was quite disgusted that we weren't expected to learn any domestic chores," he told her as he thanked her for her help. "But my father explained that it would have shocked the staff if we showed up in the kitchens expecting to cook our own meals or the laundry room to clean our clothes. My brother, Merrick, and I got off easy. Our stepsister, Miri, wasn't so lucky. When she joined our family, she learned the consequences of being stepdaughter to a king. Poor thing."

Juliana cupped her chin in her hand and gazed at him across the candlelit table. "Why poor thing?"

He shrugged. "She found it difficult to deal with the restrictions and all the protocol." His brows drew together. "Wasn't there a movie a while back along those lines? Something about an American girl who discovers she's a princess and has to learn how to act the part?"

"I remember it. Cute movie."

"Well, Miri lived it. Merrick and I had been trained for our roles since birth. Miri was seven when she came to live with us. It took a while before she fit in. And Merrick and I didn't make it easy for her, either. At least, not at first."

Something in his tone roused her curiosity. "What happened to change that?"

Lander's mouth compressed. "Merrick and I overheard someone telling her that she wasn't a 'real' princess. It was true, of course. She wasn't a princess. But I don't think she understood that until then. I'll never forget the expression on her face. It devastated her. From that moment on, Merrick and I closed ranks. She was our sister, if not by birth then by choice, and we weren't about to let anyone hurt her like that again. When my father discovered what happened, he adopted her and had her crowned Princess Miri."

"What a wonderful thing to do," Juliana marveled.

"My father was an amazing man." Lander's declaration held equal parts love and sorrow. "Not a day goes by that I don't miss him. I can only hope that if I'm elected I'll make half the king he did."

"I'm sure you will."

"Thanks for the vote of confidence, but everything considered, it won't be easy. Verdonia is facing some challenging times."

It didn't take much to read between the lines. "I've heard rumors about the amethysts. There's growing concern that the mines are played out. What will happen if it's true? Aren't the gems Verdonia's economic mainstay?"

"We'll find alternatives to help bolster the economy.

I'm considering a number of possibilities." Determination filled his expression. "It might take a while, but we're a strong people. We'll adapt."

Juliana lowered her gaze, a puzzle piece clicking into place. She'd wondered why Joc had come to Verdonia. He'd claimed it was to see her, to pressure her back into her old job. But she'd had trouble buying that. Now she suspected she had the answer. If Verdonia faced financial difficulties, who better to call in than financial wizard Joc Arnaud?

She didn't have long to dwell on the matter. Lander leaned forward and took her hand in his. "So, tell me, Juliana. Have you made a decision?"

His question caught her by surprise. "About what?"

"About tonight. Do you want an out?"

Didn't he know? Hadn't he sensed her decision? "I don't need an out." She fixed him with an unwavering look. "I'm staying."

"In that case, let's try a little experiment." Releasing her hand, he rose and crossed to her side. When she would have stood to join him, he pressed her back into her chair. "No, no. You don't need to move. Just sit for a minute."

"What are you going to do?" she asked, torn between apprehension and amusement.

"Just this." He released the clip anchoring her hair at the nape of her neck and filled his hands with the curls that tumbled free. "Soft. And much prettier loose."

"It's too curly." Her voice had grown thick and heavy. "It gets in the way."

"It won't get in my way."

His hands drifted downward to her neck, circling her throat. Sliding his palms along the lapels of her suit coat, he reached the first button and flicked it through the hole. One by one, he released them until the jacket parted. Still standing behind her, he turned his attention to her blouse. Again he took his time, unfastening button after button.

Her breath quickened with each one he loosened, and she fisted her hands around the arms of her chair. It seemed to take forever before he finished. Was he waiting for her to protest? To change her mind? It wouldn't happen. It was as though her inhibitions were released with each practiced flick, freeing her to express every sensation crashing through her. At long last he finished, sliding both jacket and blouse from her body.

"Nice," he commented, tracing the scalloped lace edging her bra. "Very nice. Who'd have guessed you were hiding something this sexy under such a prim business suit? Which is the truth, do you suppose? The suit or the lingerie?"

"What makes you think they're not both the truth?"

His index finger dipped beneath the lace and stroked. "Are they? Or is one truer than the other? Siren or businesswoman? Which is the better fit?"

"This morning, trying to change a baby's life, it was the businesswoman. Although I'm not sure that's even an accurate description. Perhaps *advocate* suits best. As for tonight…"

She stood, praying her legs would hold her. The instant she turned to face him, he kicked the chair out of the way. "What about tonight?" he asked.

"I'm not a siren. But I am a woman, a woman who wants you." She stepped closer. "You're wasting time. Are you going to take me or just talk about it?"

Four

Lander didn't need any further prompting. He swept Juliana into his arms and carried her to the bedroom. He didn't bother turning on the lights. A half-moon shone through the windows offering the perfect amount of illumination. He released her legs and allowed her to slide down his body, inch by luscious inch. The moon turned her into a palette of charcoal and silver—skin kissed with silver moonbeams, eyes as inky as the coal-black sky. Even her hair picked up the shades of the night, dousing the flames, if not the heat the color imitated.

He lowered his head, burying a kiss in the silken juncture of shoulder and throat. "One night," he whispered against her heated skin. "I swear I'll make it unforgettable."

He could feel her hands on his head, her fingers trembling as she threaded them into his hair. "I want unforgettable," she told him, holding him close. "Even more, I want to give it to you, as well."

"You already have."

He feathered kisses across her face, determined to taste every part of her. He was so intent on his exploration that he barely felt her unbutton his shirt or loosen his belt buckle. He fought against the urge to take, quickly and thoroughly. Juliana deserved more. If they only had one night, he would make certain they took their time and enjoyed every single second.

He found the zip at the side of her skirt and lowered it. To his amusement she rested her hands on his shoulders, and gave a rolling shimmy that sent the skirt drifting to the floor before nudging it aside. It left her standing in a pool of moonlight, clad in stockings and heels and a bra and thong. She paused then, and he caught a hint of vulnerability in her upturned face.

He traced her cheekbones with his thumbs. "What's wrong?"

"Nothing. I mean—" She made a small, fluttering gesture. "Nothing's wrong, exactly. It's just that I've known you barely a day."

"And yet you're standing in my bedroom, practically nude, about to make love to me."

He could feel a flush gather along her cheeks. "Yes."

"And it feels wrong."

"No." She shivered from the sudden chill that seemed to have invaded the room. Instead of wrapping her arms around herself or reaching for her clothes, as he half expected her to do, she shifted deeper into his arms, drawing warmth from him. "It feels right. It scares me how right it feels. How could that be in just a few short hours?"

She'd stunned him with her confession. Even more

unnerving was how her observation mirrored his own subconscious thoughts. Holding her, loving her, having her in his bed, his apartment, his life, did feel right. It wasn't a possibility he was willing to deal with, not when they only had this one night available to them.

This rightness, it had to result from the novelty of the situation. No more than that. Just lust. Once sated it would diminish, easing from this clawing necessity to something more manageable. Something that didn't tear him apart inside. Years from now when this time with Juliana came to mind, he'd smile reminiscently, savoring the faded memory the same way he savored a fine port or a Cuban cigar.

He glanced down at the woman he held, certain their reaction to each other was simple sexual attraction. How could it be anything more? Resolution filled him. He'd make the most of what they shared in the next few hours. Give her a memory she'd never forget, something she could savor, as well. And then it would end.

"It feels right because it is right," he reassured. For now. Knowing he had to be fair, he added, "We can stop. If it's only sex, it'll pass. We'll come to our senses, eventually." Maybe.

She laughed at that. "I don't think this will pass, not until we've done something about it."

Nor did he. "Then let's see how right we can make it."

There wasn't any talking after that. Focus narrowed, tightened. He could sense the slow build within her, the gradual drift from sweet want to desperate need. He curbed his impatience, the instinct to take her fast and thoroughly. To mark her as his. Instead, he continued on a slow, languid path, savoring each progressive step.

He unhooked her bra while she made short work of

his unbuttoned shirt. His slacks came next, along with her heels. He knelt to roll her stockings down the endless length of her legs, pausing periodically to kiss the path the drift of silk bared.

She clung to him for balance, shuddering beneath his caresses. "Hurry," she urged.

"Not a chance." He gave his undivided attention to the inner curve of her thigh, catching her as she sagged in his arms. "This is too important to rush."

Clothes ringed them in a tangled circle. Snatching a final kiss, he lifted her into his arms. He stepped from the circle of clothes and moonlight toward the shadowed bed, following her down onto the plush comforter. Her dark curls flowed out around her, captivating him. She was one of the most beautiful women he'd ever seen. Satin soft. Warm and generous. Filled with a hunger that matched his own. She returned his look, seducing him with a laugh as she melted against him.

"What would make you happy, love?" He filled his palms with her breasts and gently nipped at the rigid tips before laving them with his tongue. "This? Or how about…"

He trailed kisses downward, over the valley of her belly to the edge of her thong. Hooking his thumbs in the elastic riding her hips, he tugged, baring her. The perfume of her sex threatened to drive him insane. He found her with his mouth. Loved her. He heard her choked cry, her pleading words escaping in swift, desperate pants. Her muscles bunched, buttocks and thighs rippling beneath the strain, while she gathered up fistfuls of the comforter. Within minutes a high keening sob broke from her and she shattered in his arms.

"No, no." Her head moved restlessly back and forth. "It can't be over."

He soothed her with a gentle touch. "It's not over, love. It's just beginning."

He covered her body with his, stroking initially to calm, then to arouse. He'd promised himself when they'd met that he'd explore every inch of her body, and tonight he intended to do just that. They exchanged kisses, tentative at first, then with growing ardor. He'd anticipated a slow burn, building bit by bit, log heaped on burning log. But it was nothing like that. Wildfire exploded, sweeping fierce and reckless in one direction then another, overrunning sense and sensibility until they were both caught up in a maelstrom beyond their control.

His hands played over her until he heard the hitch in her breath that warned of her approaching climax. He sought out the heart of her, cupping the source of the fire. He'd done this to her. His touch had brought her to the brink once again. The knowledge roused something indescribable in him, awakening an emotion he couldn't put name to or fully understand. It was primal and viscerally male. A word echoed in the deepest recesses of his mind. A single word, chanted over and over again, like a mantra, offering both promise and intent.

Mine.

Juliana's voice joined the chorus. "Please. Please, Lander. Take me now. Make me yours."

He levered above her and dipped himself in her liquid heat. She wrapped her legs around him, locking him tightly against her. He surged, deep and hard, stroking into her. He'd never in his life felt anything like it. So snug and sleek. Almost virginal. She gasped out his name and when he moved even that one word was lost to her.

Still, he heard her singing, a soft musical cry of urgency and delight. Of wonder. Of rapture. And somehow he knew—knew without doubt or question—that it was a song she'd never sung before. That the woman in his arms wasn't almost virginal. Until just seconds ago, she'd been a virgin. She'd given herself to him without condition or hesitation, despite there being no future in it for either of them.

He mated their bodies, filling her again and again, whispering words, endless words, he couldn't afterward recall. They poured from the very heart of him as he poured his heart and soul into her. She arched beneath him, and the building came, faster and more powerful than before. It pounded unrelentingly until they reached the dizzying crest, teetering there for an endless second. The climax came, so hard and merciless, that all they could do was surrender to its taking, clinging to each other in its aftermath.

Breathless, they collapsed in a tangle of slick arms and legs, utterly spent. He had no idea how long they lay there while their bodies cooled, then chilled. Flinging out a hand, Lander snagged a section of comforter and pulled it over them, cocooning them in a silken nest.

Forever passed before passion eased and his brain began to function again. "Why, Juliana?" He rolled onto his side, levering himself upward onto an elbow. "Why didn't you tell me?"

To his frustration the bed remained in shadow, concealing her expression. Even so, he could hear the wariness in her voice. "Tell you what?"

"Don't pretend. You've never done anything like this before. Why now? Why me?"

She shrugged. "Because it felt right."

"That's not good enough."

She sat up, and this time the moon did find her, cutting across her face and lapping over her bared shoulders. "Do you think I wanted it to be you? That I wasn't hoping for more than you have to offer? More than I can give you? But when you touch me…" She turned her face away. "Is it just me? Or do you feel it, too? Isn't that why I'm here?"

"Hell. I'm sorry." He snagged a rope of curls and tugged until she looked at him again. "It just caught me by surprise. I find it hard to believe that there hasn't been a man in your life before this."

"There was a man."

A possessive stab caught Lander by surprise. "Obviously things didn't work out, because there's no question in my mind that he never had you in his bed."

"No." The intense pain in that single word had him wanting to gather her up and protect her from everyone and everything that might hurt her again. "He wanted to seduce me for reasons of his own. I found out before I made the ultimate mistake."

Possessiveness turned to cold anger. "A Verdonian?"

"No, Your Highness." A hint of gold flickered in her eyes, highlighting her amusement. "Not a Verdonian. The dungeons and torture rooms won't be needed."

"I'd have done it," he growled.

"Let's forget about Stewart." She rolled on top of him and captured his mouth with hers. "Isn't there something else you'd rather be doing?"

It was an offer he couldn't resist. The remaining hours of the night flowed from one unforgettable moment into another until exhaustion overtook them and they finally slept. When next Lander awoke, sunlight enveloped the room, filling it with a sparkling brilliance. But the warmth had fled.

Juliana was gone.

Juliana lifted her face to the first rays of the morning sun. Rather than hail a cab, she decided to walk for a while, needing the exercise to help center herself. Initially, her steps were light and joyous, the blood singing through her veins. Last night was the most incredible of her life. She'd never imagined lovemaking could be so earth-shattering. The fact that one man could make her feel so loved and cherished, amazed her every bit as much as it confused her. But Lander had done that and more.

A secret smile swept across her mouth and a passing pedestrian returned the smile with a wink and a grin. She shook her head, marveling. Imagine a lifetime filled with nights like the one she'd just experienced. Greeting each day locked in Lander's arms, having the right to stay there as long as she wanted. And imagine waking each morning filled with a jubilance and contentment that surpassed anything she'd dared believe possible. She hugged the emotions close, reveling in them.

Until she remembered.

Lander could never be a part of her life. She'd never know what it felt like to awaken in his arms, because it would never happen. She'd agreed to give him a single night, no more. And he'd accepted the offer and promised not to ask for another. Even if he wanted to see her again, to continue their relationship, it was impossible.

Maybe he'd have succeeded in tempting her if he could have guaranteed that their affair would remain secret. But she'd had enough experience with the paparazzi to know better. Eventually they'd discover Lander was seeing her. And once they did, they'd ferret out her identity. Her real identity. When that happened, it would cost Lander big-time. He might very well lose the election because of her and she couldn't bear it if that happened. Besides it wasn't like she'd be staying in Verdonia much longer. Soon she'd move on to another European country.

Her energy drained away, her earlier euphoria fizzling like a spent firecracker. Hailing a cab, she sat in the back, fighting tears. She tried to run through a series of mathematical equations to calm herself, but even that was beyond her. Ten minutes later she arrived outside of her apartment building. Paying the driver, she entered the complex and took the elevator to the tenth floor, grateful that she had no work pending and could take the day off to lick her wounds. To her dismay, even that was denied her. Stepping into her apartment, she found Joc waiting. She took one look at her brother and burst into tears.

"Aw, hell," he muttered, gathering her into his arms. "What did that bastard do to you?"

"Nothing. Everything." She fought to regain control with only limited success. "I'm sorry, Joc. I don't know what's the matter with me."

"I told you to stay away from him. Naturally you didn't listen and now he's made you cry." Beneath the brotherly concern she heard a ferocity that alarmed her. "No one's made you cry since Stewart."

His comment stopped her cold. She remembered all too well what he'd done to Stewart for that single affront. The only jobs still available to him involved mops and buckets of soapy water.

"No!" She pulled back, fisting her hands in her brother's shirt. "Now you listen up, big brother. You stay out of this. Lander didn't make me cry. I'm serious. He didn't."

He greeted her reassurance with skepticism. "Then why are you so upset?"

"Because he wanted to continue the relationship and I refused to even consider it."

It wasn't precisely accurate, but she didn't doubt for a minute that if she'd made the offer, Lander would have accepted without hesitation. He'd wanted her to stay with him. The desire had been buried in every whispered word, in each hungry kiss, in his first tender caress, straight through to his last. He'd overwhelmed her with want, seduced her with a need she'd never realized she possessed. If she'd been able to find the least little excuse for remaining with him, she'd have seized it without hesitation. But there hadn't been any reasonable excuses. The risk was too great, protecting Lander's reputation paramount. That far outweighed her petty wishes.

Joc shook his head. "You're not making a bit of sense. That alone is peculiar, considering you're one of the most rational, analytical women I know. If Lander still wants you, then what's the problem?"

"You know what the problem is."

A muscle jerked in his jaw. "You're afraid people will find out who you are and dig up old history about you. And you don't want to be in that sort of media frenzy again."

"Yes." She let go of his shirt, trying to smooth the wrinkles as assiduously as she tried to smooth the pain from her face. "You were right to warn me away from him. He's a prince. I'm no one. I'm worse than no one.

If his people find out who I am or about my background, he'll lose the election."

"You don't know that, not for sure," he protested.

"Yes, I do." She took a step back and offered her most implacable expression, the one she used when dealing with recalcitrant clients. "It's over, Joc. I had my one night with him. That's all I asked for or wanted, and it's exactly what I received." It would be foolish to hope for more.

"Are you certain? I can fix this, if you want."

"I'm positive. And no, I don't want you to fix a thing." She managed a quick, bright smile. "Seriously. Stay out of it."

Joc met her smile with one of his own, his a hard flash of white against his sun-darkened skin. "Okay, Ana." He tucked a tumble of curls behind her ear. "After all, haven't I always given you everything you wanted?"

"Yes, you have." But he couldn't help her this time, she realized. What she wanted wasn't his to give.

The instant the door closed behind her brother, the dam broke and with it came the realization that by allowing herself to become emotionally involved with the one man she couldn't have, she'd totally and completely ruined her life.

Lander stared at Arnaud in stunned disbelief. "What did you say?"

"You heard me." Determination was carved into every line of Joc's face. "I want you to marry my sister. In fact, our negotiations hinge on that very point."

Lander sliced his hand through the air, cutting him off. "Forget it. Maybe if you'd approached me a week ago. *Maybe* I'd have considered it. I'm that desperate. But not now."

"Because of Juliana."

He hadn't felt this possessive toward a woman ever. "Yes, because of Juliana."

"I thought it was a one-night stand."

"You bastard! Did she tell you that?"

"I have no intention of betraying her confidence." A hint of mockery crept into Joc's voice. "As far as I'm concerned you have two choices. I can either beat you to a bloody pulp for messing with Juliana, or I can make you pay for what you did to her by forcing you to give up your precious freedom. Personally, whaling on you for a bit holds far more appeal."

In two strides Lander was across the room and had Joc by the throat and up against the nearest wall. "What's your relationship with her?" he demanded. "She swore you weren't lovers, something I can verify as fact. So, why are you throwing up roadblocks between us? Why put your sister in the middle of all this? You want Juliana for yourself, don't you?"

To Lander's surprise Joc didn't try and break his hold. "I want Juliana to be happy."

"And marrying your sister will make her happy?" That didn't make sense.

"I believe so." Joc actually had the nerve to laugh. "Why don't I show you a picture of my sister."

"What the hell good will that do?" He released Joc with an exclamation of disgust. "You think I'm going to take one look at her and fall madly in love?"

Joc shrugged. "It could happen." He removed a snapshot from his wallet and spun it in Lander's direction. "Why don't we try it and see."

Lander caught the photo midair. Flipping it over, he stared at the picture in sheer disbelief.

"My sister. Juliana Rose Arnaud. I always called her Ana." Joc shrugged. "I guess the nickname carries bad memories, so she doesn't use it anymore."

It took Lander two tries before he could speak. "This has been a setup from the beginning, hasn't it?" He shot Joc a furious glare. "I call you for help and who shows up at the ball while I'm waiting for you, but your sister—a sister who's conveniently forgotten her last name's Arnaud. She falls into my arms like a ripe peach and after we spend one unforgettable night together all of a sudden I find out the two of you are related. And coincidence of all coincidences, the very next day you're holding our contract for ransom."

Joc shook his head. "Clever plan. I wish I could actually take credit for it. But I can't, because it didn't go down that way."

"I don't care how it went down. I suggest you get the hell out of Verdonia while you still have your head attached to your shoulders."

Joc held up a hand in an appeasing gesture. "Look, I swear there was no setup. I tried to warn her about you, Montgomery. I can't tell you how many times I advised her to give you a wide berth. But Juliana has a soft spot for jackals like you and once your relationship took a turn for the worse, this seemed an obvious solution."

"Not to me."

A hint of anger glittered in Joc's black gaze. "Maybe you should have thought of that before your North Pole got overruled by the southern half of your equator. Now let's talk turkey because this is how it's going down. I'm making a one-time offer. You refuse, I walk. And your precious country can go bankrupt for all I care."

Son of a— "What do you want?"

"Your end of our business arrangement is simple. Get my sister to fall in love with you. Should be easy since she's halfway there already. Marry her. Treat her like the queen she deserves to be. Live happily ever after. Hell, have babies if you're so inclined." He paused, shooting Lander a keen look. "Think you can do that?"

Babies? An image of redheaded toddlers racing through the palace came all too easily to mind. He took a step back, mentally and literally. "I think you're interfering where you don't belong."

The two locked gazes for an endless minute. "But you'll do it, won't you?" Joc demanded. "You'd do anything to save your country, including marry my sister."

Lander ground his teeth in silent fury. "Yes," he finally bit out.

"Even if it means being related to me?" Joc pressed harder. "And even if our connection causes you to lose the election?"

It very well might. Lander turned away and allowed the possibility to settle into his heart and mind. Not that it took much thought. He'd seen Arnaud's plan for Verdonia. It was a good one, one that had an excellent shot at ensuring full financial recovery. Setup or not, if the price he had to pay for that was marriage, he'd do it. If it meant saving Verdonia from economic disaster, he'd have married a two-headed goat, and Juliana was far from that.

Still, he didn't like Joc's tactics anymore than he liked suspecting someone as open and candid as Juliana of deceit. Granted, she'd concealed her full name from him, but he had a feeling that was a one-time aberration. What he liked least of all was being forced to marry on command. He'd always been the one in charge of his own destiny. He'd always been the one to command. It rankled more than a little to play puppet to Joc's puppeteer.

Turning, he asked, "I gather she's not to know about the addendum to our contract?"

"That would be a definite deal breaker."

It confirmed Lander's suspicion that if this was a setup, Juliana had played the part of unwitting pawn. "Just one question." He approached. "Why? You can't honestly believe this is in your sister's best interest?"

He didn't think Arnaud would answer. Emotions swept across the Texan's face. Anger. Stubborn determination. And—hell, could it be?—an odd vulnerability. "You're wrong, Montgomery," he said at last. "This is in her best interest. I couldn't protect her growing up. I'm not even much good at protecting her now." His expression hardened. "But you can do what I can't. You can give her everything she needs, everything I've never been able to."

Lander wanted to argue the point. This was a huge mistake, one he didn't doubt he'd live long to regret. But he didn't see any other choice. He wanted to explain what a disservice it was to Juliana to be married for financial gain rather than love. That she wouldn't appreciate this sort of manipulation any more than he did. But he knew from long experience that once Arnaud set his mind to something, he was impossible to budge. There might be room for negotiation later on, a better opportunity to apply calm reason to reckless obsession. Until then, Lander had no choice.

"Do we have a deal?" Joc asked impatiently.

"Yes, it's a deal."

He took Arnaud's hand in a tight grip, grinding bone against bone as he fixed the man with a fierce stare.

"Someday you'll find yourself boxed into a corner like this. Remember me when that happens, Arnaud. Remember, and know that you brought it on yourself when you forced this agreement on the woman you should have protected, and the one man who will do whatever it takes to see that you pay for your arrogance."

Five

Juliana finished the last of her paperwork, signing her name with a swift practiced stroke, before shoving the folder to one side of her desk. Swiveling to face the window, she leaned back in her chair and closed her eyes. Exhaustion threatened to overwhelm her. The past three days had been hideous, perhaps because she'd chosen to work nonstop rather than pacing herself. But at least it had kept her from obsessing over Lander and that one unforgettable night.

A knock sounded at her door, and she stifled a groan. The clock on the wall warned it was well past seven. The office staff should have long since cleared out, with the possible exception of her assistant. She heard him push open the door but didn't bother to open her eyes. "Colin, I thought I told you to go home an hour ago," she complained. Her assistant didn't answer, but she could hear him approach, no doubt to get the last of the papers she'd signed. "Didn't you have a date tonight?"

To her shock, he put his hands on her, his fingers digging into the knots of tension ridging her shoulders. Her eyes blinked open and she shot straight up in her chair. "Good Lord. Colin?"

"Gone."

"Lander!" She swiveled around, staring up at him in disbelief. "What are you doing here?"

"I came to see you, of course."

He plucked her out of the chair and into his arms. For an instant she allowed herself to relax against him before common sense prevailed and she fought her way free of his hold. "Please don't take this the wrong way, but…why?"

"Because of this."

Lowering his head, he teased her mouth with his. She had every intention of stopping him, of pulling back from those coaxing lips. Of telling him firmly and un-equivocally that she had no interest in seeing him ever again. Her good intentions lasted all of two seconds.

With a groan she gave up and fell into the embrace. She twined her arms around his neck and practically inhaled him. He walked her backward the two paces to her desk and lifted her onto the wooden surface. Her skirt hitched upward and he planted his hands on her knees and parted them. Stepping between, he tugged her tight against him.

"What are we doing?" she demanded, torn between laughter and tears.

"What we were meant to do."

"We agreed to a single night."

"Your choice, not mine. And like a fool, I didn't push

hard enough." He broke off to kiss her again, deep, drugging kisses. "But I've decided I want to renegotiate the terms of that agreement."

She started shaking her head before he'd finished speaking. "No. No, I can't. You have to trust that I have an excellent reason. Several of them, actually."

"Give me one."

She struggled to balance truth with caution. "You have an election coming up. You need to focus on that."

"My personal life has never interfered with my duty to my country. You should know, that takes primary importance over everything. Always," he emphasized. Sweeping the clip from her hair, he forked his fingers through the mass of curls. "But that doesn't mean I don't have time for you, as well. What's your next excuse for ending our relationship?"

"A point of clarity, if you don't mind. We don't have a relationship."

He merely smiled. His hands dropped to her legs, sliding upward, gathering her skirt as he went. "Tell me what you call it."

She shuddered beneath his touch, struggling to maintain an ounce of reason in the midst of this insanity. "A one-night stand."

His grip tightened on her thighs. "Don't." The single word sounded harsh, almost guttural. "Don't denigrate what happened between us."

"I'm just being honest." She struggled to tidy a messy situation, regardless of the pain it caused. To fit it neatly into its appropriately labeled box, a sealed box etched with "one-night stand" on the lid in indelible marker. "And though I can't explain all the problems it will cause if we continue to see each other, it's important you believe me. That you believe that it's best for Verdonia."

He dismissed her assertion with a shrug. "Why don't you let me decide that. There's only one question you need to answer. Was our one night together enough?"

She closed her eyes, dropping her head to his shoulder. "Please don't ask me that."

"Too late." She could feel his smile against the side of her neck. "Be honest, Juliana. You want more, just as I do."

The temptation to admit the truth was overwhelming. "Yes," she whispered. "I want more. But I'm begging you to walk away. There's so much you don't know about me."

His mouth traced a path along her neck to a sweet spot just beneath her ear. "In time, when you learn to trust me, you can tell me all your secrets."

Didn't he understand? With an effort, she lifted her head to look at him. "You're better off not knowing."

"At some point you'll tell me." He repeated the assertion with casual certainty. "You won't have any choice."

"You're probably right." She released her breath in a sigh. "If I agree, there are conditions."

"Name them."

"No one can know about us. And I mean no one."

"Agreed. Next."

"No falling in love."

To her surprise, that gave him pause. "You think you can order love? Where have I heard that before?"

"I don't know." Where had he? "But we can try."

"Sex and nothing but sex?"

It sounded so crude. So harsh. Not that she had any other option. She couldn't afford to fall in love with Lander. "Would that be so wrong?"

"Yes." He lifted her chin, forcing her to meet his

green-flecked eyes. She caught a hint of amusement, softened by tenderness. "Yes, it's wrong. But you'll need to discover that for yourself. What other conditions do you have?"

She hadn't a clue what else. Maybe if she'd anticipated this conversation, she'd have had a list prepared. Neatly numbered and bulleted, of course. But she'd ended things between them. She distinctly remembered doing it, even though it had ripped her apart. She'd cried over him and everything. And yet here he was, standing between her thighs with her skirt hiked to her hips and eighty-six combined inches of leg locked around his waist.

She shook her head. "I don't know. I'll give you the rest when I can think straight."

"In that case, I'm not sure I want you thinking straight." To her surprise, his grip firmed on her hips, pulling her so tightly against him that his belt buckle bit into her abdomen. "If that's everything, I suggest we get on with it."

"Excuse me?" She wriggled in discomfort. "You can't mean—"

"I do mean," he confirmed. "Right here and right now."

Had he gone crazy? She eyed him uncertainly. "Some women might want to make love on top of a desk, but I'm not one of them."

"Really?" A slight smile curved his lips and his gaze ran over her, lingering. "What happened to sex and nothing but sex?"

She became vividly aware of how she must look, her hair rioting around her shoulders, her skirt flipped back to expose everything from her waist down, her legs clasped about him. Heat scored her cheekbones and she had trouble meeting his gaze. "Not here," she whispered. "Not like this."

"I don't understand. I thought you said it's just sex, no emotion involved." He ran the tip of his finger over the swell of her breast. He'd touched her in a similar manner on a number of occasions, but this time it felt different. Careless. Distant. Carnal. "It's not like we need a bed. We can do it right here." He glanced around. "Or up against the wall over there. Or on the floor. Rug burns, but what the hell. I'm hungry, I eat. Isn't that how it works?"

She unwound her legs from his waist and shoved at his shoulders. Not that it did any good. He remained as unyielding as granite. "Please, move. I want to get off the desk."

"I'm serious, Juliana. Explain it to me. What does it matter where?" His hands dropped to her thighs. "Or how?"

She covered his hands with hers, attempting to stop those clever fingers from exploring any further. To her horror, tears pricked her eyes and her throat closed over, making it a struggle to respond. "It just does, okay?"

His hold eased. Gentled. Cupping her face, he leaned forward and kissed her. "And that, my beautiful Juliana, proves my point. Sex alone will never be enough for either of us because it's innately wrong." Stepping back, he helped her off the desk. With a few swift tugs, he straightened her clothing. "I'm sorry if I upset you."

She wobbled on her heels, struggling to regain her composure. "If that's how you feel—that it can't just be about sex, then why did you agree when I suggested it?"

He shot her a wicked look. "Oh, I'd have been willing to give it a try, if you insisted."

"Magnanimous of you," she muttered.

"I thought so." His smile faded. "But in the end, we'd have failed."

"And one of us would have gotten hurt." She rested her head against his shoulder. "So why are we doing this?"

His arms slid around her. "Because we don't have any other choice."

He made it sound as though fate had set something in motion, something they could neither change nor escape, assuming they wanted to. She felt a sudden urge to run. To return with Joc to Dallas. She was good at running. She'd done it often enough. Her breath trembled in a sigh. She'd done it often enough to know it never worked. If people wanted to find you, they could. If they wanted to expose you, they did.

Chances were, running and hiding wouldn't work this time, either. But until the truth came out—and it always came out—she'd enjoy however much time she had with Lander and hope it was enough. It would have to be.

"So what now?" she asked.

"Now we play."

She glanced up at him, intrigued. "Play?"

"You look confused. Haven't you ever played before?"

She thought about it before slowly shaking her head. "Not really."

"Then it's past time you started."

The nights following flew by as though part of a dream. During the daylight, Juliana worked harder than she thought possible so she could enjoy those few precious nighttime hours with Lander. It became like a game. Late each afternoon she'd receive a phone call giving her a different location to meet, each in a section of the city free from curious eyes. And every evening she'd escape work and race to wherever she'd been directed.

She always found a different vehicle waiting for her, the only thing they had in common a unifying anonymity in appearance that guaranteed they'd fade in with every other car on the busy streets of Mt. Roche.

The first night she was driven to an underground garage, and had expected to find herself back at the apartment complex where she'd made love to Lander. But that hadn't happened. Instead, she ended up in one of the downtown malls. Even though all the shops were lit, to her astonishment not a soul stirred. She and Lander spent the entire night wandering through the mall, laughing at the insanity of having the entire place to themselves. Every once in a while she'd catch a glimpse of the security guards who shadowed their every move. She hadn't noticed them the night she'd spent at his apartment, but she had an uneasy feeling they'd been there, regardless.

Most of the time she could ignore their presence and dart from store to store, trying on clothes or jewelry or shoes, or wandering through the bookstores or among the craft stalls. Just as exhaustion set in, dinner miraculously appeared at a small table inside a trendy café. They dined by candlelight, soft music playing in the background. When they'd finished, Lander escorted her back to the car she'd arrived in, which, to her astonishment, delivered her home again.

The next night Lander arranged for a private showing at a movie theater. Another evening found them wandering through a wild animal park on the outskirts of the city. He took her ice skating. Swimming. He even arranged for a night at a spa. But not once did he take her back to the apartment and make love to her as she longed for him to do.

He must have been aware of her confusion, just as he must have been aware of how much she wanted to be in his arms again. She didn't understand it. As impossible as it seemed, it was almost as though he were… wooing her. But that didn't make a bit of sense.

On the tenth night, her car pulled into another underground garage. Once again she thought perhaps it was the apartment complex, and hope flared. But when she stepped from the vehicle, one of Lander's private bodyguards whisked her along a set of unfamiliar corridors dotted with security. He paused before a heavy steel door, guarded by his hulking counterpart.

Opening the door, he gestured for her to enter. "Please go on through, Ms. Rose," he said. "Tell His Highness that I'm here if he needs anything."

Before she could ask the guard where she was, the door clanged shut behind her. Subdued lighting suffused the room, and it took a minute for her eyes to adjust. Once they had, she was astonished to discover she stood in a museum.

"It's one of my favorite places to come." Lander spoke from the shadows across the room. He flicked on a light switch, flooding the room with a brighter glow. "Do you like museums?"

"Yes," she confessed. "Very much."

"This one has it all. Art. History. Science."

The hours flowed one into the next as he led her through each wing. As they explored the section detailing Verdonia's rich history, Lander brought it to life with stories that gave added depth and color to each exhibit. Later, they ate picnic-style on the floor in front of a

Monet and a Renoir with a Rodin sculpture guarding them from the corner. And they talked, endlessly.

The evening concluded in a small secure room housing the crown jewels of Verdonia. "The ones not in use," Lander teased.

To her astonishment, he opened the cases and lifted out various pieces for her to try on. "I'm afraid to touch them," she told him. "I half expect your guards to burst in here and arrest me."

"I have to admit, you're the first woman outside the royals who's ever had the opportunity to do this." He fastened a necklace dripping with diamonds and amethysts around her neck. "What do you think?"

Mirrors lined the back of each display case and she stood in front of one to look, watching the gems dance and glitter with her every breath. "It's stunning."

"It was a wedding gift from my father to my mother, along with these." He lifted out a tiara and settled it in her curls. Then he slipped a ring on her finger, the central stone a huge amethyst, the purplish-blue depths flashing with red fire. "This ring's called Soul Mate, which is actually what the Verdonia Royal symbolizes."

"Verdonia Royal? Is that what the amethyst is called?"

"That particular color. There's not another shade quite like it anywhere else in the world. We also have pink stones which are far more common, but popular, nonetheless."

"A Rose de France? I've heard of them."

He glared at her in mock anger. "Please. Celestia Blush."

She swept him a deep, graceful courtesy. "I beg your pardon, Your Highness. I misspoke. I swear it won't happen again."

"See that it doesn't."

Rising, she studied the circle of Blushes that surrounded the Royal. "Does the Blush have a special meaning, too?"

Lander nodded. "It signifies the sealing of a contract. When it's set in a circle like this it denotes a binding agreement, in this case a marriage."

"It's beautiful." She glanced at him hesitantly. "You must miss your mother very much."

"She died when I was very young, Merrick little more than a baby. My memories are more…impressions. Feelings of warmth and comfort."

His expression remained open, so she risked another question. "You said it took a while to adjust to your stepsister's advent in your life. What about your stepmother's?"

"She's an impressive lady." An odd smile curved his mouth. "Did you know she designed her own engagement ring?"

"Really? What does it look like?"

"There's a replica of it over here."

She joined him in front of a display case and stared at the ring. It was quite different from the one belonging to Lander's mother. Three gem stones—a diamond, an emerald and a ruby—made up the central portion of the ring, the trio surrounded by a circle of alternating Verdonia Royals and sapphires.

"It means something, doesn't it?"

"Yes." A poignant quality had crept into his voice. "And once Merrick and I figured it out, we became a family."

"Birthstones?"

"Clever, Juliana. Yes, they're birthstones. The three in the center represent Merrick, Miri and me. All of them are of exact equal weight, cut and clarity."

"And the circle of amethysts and sapphires? Your father and stepmother?"

"The amethyst, ironically enough, is my stepmother's birthstone. The sapphire, my father's. And if you look carefully at the gold filigree that makes up the rest of the ring, it spells out two words in Verdonian."

It took Juliana a moment to find the words hidden in the pattern. "Love and…unity?"

"A circle of love and unity around the three most precious people in their lives. She's a special woman, my stepmother." He paused a beat. "You'd enjoy meeting her, as she would you."

His comment brought her down to earth with painful swiftness. Her reflection bounced back from a dozen different mirrors, mocking her. She stood in fantasy, arrayed in jewels she had no right to wear. A tiara worn by a queen. A necklace given as a royal wedding gift. A ring that connected two soul mates.

It hurt. It hurt to know that she would never be the recipient of such gifts. Oh, not the gems. She didn't care about those. It was the love and commitment and promise they stood for. Perhaps the women in her family were never meant to know those things. Certainly, her mother had never received as much from her father, though she'd kept hoping against hope, right up until her death.

Without a word Juliana turned her back on Lander, at the same time turning her back on a reflection that was just that—a reflection of reality. "I don't think I can work the clasp," she said, relieved that she sounded so calm. With luck she'd concealed her inner turmoil. "Would you mind?"

"Are you certain? I thought we could—"

She rounded on him, not so calm anymore, the

turmoil slipping from her control and spilling loose. "Could what? Indulge in a little make-believe? Were you going to put on a crown and play Prince Charming to my Cinderella again?"

He twined a length of her hair around his fingers. The curls clung to him like the roses had clung to a midnight arbor in a dream they'd shared on a night not long ago. "I've hurt you. I'm sorry. That wasn't my intention."

Pain threatened to overwhelm her, and it took a full minute to recover her equilibrium. "Thank you for a lovely evening, but it's time for me to return home now."

Home. Not that she actually had one. Her Verdonian apartment wasn't a true home. An image of a Texas hacienda flashed through her mind, filling her with a vague yearning. Nor was Dallas. Not any longer. She'd lost all that at the tender age of eight. Her mouth twisted. Or rather, she'd lost the illusion then. The pretense of hearth and home.

Without a word he reached behind her and unclasped the necklace. The tiara proved more problematic, tangling in curls that seemed reluctant to part with it. When she would have yanked it free, Lander stopped her, gently coaxing it loose.

"There," he said at last, dropping a kiss on top of her head. "Not a single hair lost."

His comment knocked her off-kilter. He hadn't been careful out of concern for the tiara, but so he wouldn't hurt her. Her breath escaped in a gusty sigh. "What are we doing? What are *you* doing?"

"Don't you know?"

She shook her head. "To be perfectly honest, I haven't a clue."

"You're a smart woman. You'll figure it out eventually."

"I don't want to figure it out eventually." She studied him, attempting to analyze the situation. She should be able to logic it out. To add it up or puzzle it through, or apply reason to the problem and come up with a simple solution. One plus one always equaled two. But no matter how hard she tried, nothing made sense. "You're playing some sort of game. I wish I knew what it was."

He paused in the process of returning the pieces of jewelry to the display cases. "This is no game."

"Are you trying to seduce me?" She shook her head as soon as she'd posed the question. "That doesn't make sense. I vaguely recall you did that already."

He lifted an eyebrow. "If it's such a vague memory, I must have done something wrong." He locked the case. "Perhaps there's another explanation. A very simple, very obvious one."

"Wait. You forgot the ring." She slipped it from her finger and held it out to him. "The only explanation that makes any sense is that you're still trying to prove that what we feel isn't lust. Like you did in my office."

He took the ring from her. But instead of returning it to the display case, he pocketed it. "Close, but not quite there."

"I give up. Tell me what's going on."

"What about love?"

He shocked her so that she couldn't think of a single thing to say. Taking her arm, he escorted her through the door protected by his bodyguards and to the car that had delivered her to the museum. The engine started with a soft purr and they exited from the garage onto a rain-slicked street. Lightning speared the sky while thunder cleared its throat. Heavy droplets pounded the front windshield, their descent as fast and dizzying as her thoughts.

In no time they pulled into a garage, and this time she recognized it as the one to his apartment. He parked the car and glanced at her. There wasn't an ounce of question in that silent look, just heated demand. She gave him her response by exiting the car and slamming the door. Then she stalked to the elevator, thunder rumbling approval with every step she took.

"It's not possible," she announced the minute they stepped from the elevator into the apartment.

A crash of thunder shook the building and Lander waited until it had died before asking, "What isn't possible?"

"True love. Fairy-tale romances. Happily ever after."

He glanced her way, the soft glow from a nearby lamp providing enough illumination to reveal his curiosity. "You don't believe in love? Or you don't believe in love at first sight?"

"I'm not sure I believe in either one," she confessed.

"Interesting, considering what happened when we met."

Her throat tightened. "What did happen, exactly?"

"Why don't I show you instead."

He lowered his head and sampled her mouth. Her lips parted beneath the onslaught. It was such a sweet joining, thorough and tender. When he would have pulled back, she thrust her fingers deep into his hair to prevent him and deepened the kiss. She couldn't deal with tender right now, couldn't handle all that it suggested about their relationship. But she'd accept thorough—accept it, as well as give it. She drank with greedy abandonment, consumed with a driving need to seize what he'd been promising for the past ten days.

The storm broke overhead, and the air quickened,

filled with an energy and electricity that fueled their taking, one of the other. It was fast. Edged with violence. A battle for supremacy between male and female. He drove her toward the bedroom just as lightning flared, turning the room a stark blue white and revealing a man pushed past reason. Exhilarated, she pushed harder.

"Show me more," she demanded, ripping at his clothing.

"Until there's no more to show." He stripped her with swift economy before dealing with the few remaining pieces of his own clothing. And then there was no more talking. The first moment of intense rapture caught them both by surprise, a swift, needy explosion of sheer ecstasy that mirrored the storm raging overhead.

"Tell me now that you don't believe in love," he demanded as he drove into her, sending her soaring again. "Deny it if you can."

Her breath caught on a sob. "I can't. You know I can't."

And as the heavens opened, flooding the earth, Juliana opened herself, heart and soul, no longer able to hide from the truth. She loved this man. Loved him more than she believed possible. It was as though her revelation gentled the storm. The thunder lost its voice, fading to a distant grumble, while the lightning flashed a soft farewell.

In that perfect moment they came together again. Slowly. Easily. With piercing sensitivity. Moving together in exquisite harmony.

Juliana closed her eyes, forced to accept the truth. They moved together in the ultimate expression of love.

Six

Lander woke, delighted to discover he still held Juliana in his arms. Rain-washed sunlight spilled across the bed and into her eyes, causing her to stir. With a gasp she sat up, one elbow just missing his jaw, the other nailing his gut with pinpoint accuracy. Whereas the night before she'd been all grace and poetry in motion, the morning turned her awkward and uncertain. He found it unbelievably endearing.

"Good morning," he said, once he could draw breath.

She gazed up at him, blinking the remnants of sweet dreams from her eyes. "I overslept, didn't I?"

"A bit." Unable to resist, he buried his hands in her hair, realizing as he did so how much he enjoyed the soft, springy texture, as well as the way the curls clung to his fingers. He gave her a slow, lingering kiss. "But if that means waking with you in my arms, rather than finding you've slipped out the door, so much the better."

"It's definitely better," she confessed with an abashed smile. "If not conducive to good work habits."

In that moment she looked as far removed from the self-confident businesswoman as he'd ever seen—not to mention the seductive siren who'd first captured his interest. He wasn't certain which aspect of her personality appealed the most. Right now he found the rumpled urchin a fascination he'd love to spend the rest of the morning exploring.

Before he could suggest it, a tiny frown crinkled her forehead. "What time is it, do you know?"

"Ten."

She nearly hyperventilated. "Work. Office. Late. Very, very late."

He shrugged, unconcerned. "Tell them you're with me."

That gave her pause, if only for an instant. At least it gave her enough time to calm down. "Wait a minute. Are you telling me that sleeping with the Prince of Verdon gives me a free pass at work?"

A smile slashed across his face. "Duke of Verdon," he corrected. "Prince of Verdonia. And I've been thinking of making it a royal decree. Any woman who sleeps with me is excused from work the next day. How does that sound?"

She inched toward the edge of the mattress. "You'll have them lining up at the palace doors."

He scooped her close before she could escape. "There's only one woman I want at my door, and that's you."

He saw the delight blossom in her face and felt the eager give of her body. She laughed up at him and that momentary indulgence completely altered her appearance. A mischievous pixie peeked through the regal facade of the Fairy Queen, and Lander found he couldn't take his eyes off her.

She was so beautiful, her eyes tilted at the corners, just enough to give them an exotic slant, while specks of gold glistened hungrily in the honey brown. The sunlight danced across the spill of auburn curls turning them to flame against the elegant angles of her face. And her body. Lord help him. Plump and rounded where it needed to be and long and lean everywhere else, with skin so milky it looked as though it had been painted on by a master artist.

His arms tightened. "Stay," he whispered. "Just this once."

"Just once? I tried just once. It didn't work, as I'm sure you recall." With a regretful sigh, she rolled away from him, and as much as it pained him, he let her go. "I'm sorry, Lander. I have to get to work."

"The children are depending on you, aren't they?"

"Yes." She gathered up her clothing and hugged the pieces to her so that all he could see was acres of leg vanishing into crumpled green silk.

He swept back the covers. "Give me a minute to dress and I'll drive you."

"No, don't bother. I'll just catch a cab back to my apartment."

"Why bother with a cab if I'm willing to do it?" It didn't surprise him when she avoided his gaze, not that he needed to see her eyes to guess what she was thinking. "It's because you're afraid someone will catch us together, isn't it?"

"Too many people already know. It's going to leak sooner or later." She did look at him then, and the pain he read there struck like a physical blow. "We don't have much longer."

He erupted from the bed and dragged on a pair of jeans, not bothering to fasten them. "We have as long as we want," he insisted, stalking toward her.

"My work in Verdonia is almost finished. I've already been up north in Avernos for six weeks. And I spent more than two months in Celestia. I may need to go back there for an additional week or so after I'm finished here, but…" She trailed off with a sigh of regret. "There are other countries. Other children. Europe's a big place."

He couldn't resist touching her. Needed to, for some reason. "How much longer here, in Mt. Roche?"

"A few days," she whispered. "Maybe a week."

"It's not enough."

"It'll have to be."

She ended the discussion by vanishing into the bathroom, emerging a short time later wearing her clothes from the night before. She'd somehow managed to tame her hair, ruthlessly knotting it at the nape of her neck. In her business suit, all neatly tucked and buttoned, she looked every inch the self-possessed professional. Lander took one look at her and all he could think about was freeing that glorious mane and rumpling her tidy suit until he'd released the heart of passion that beat within the woman of calm reason standing before him.

"I'll send a car for you tonight," he said.

She caught her lower lip between her teeth. "Maybe we should take a night off. I'm getting behind on my work and—"

"Your work isn't going anywhere."

"No, it isn't," she conceded. "But the children are hurt by any delay."

Hell. She'd gotten him with that one. "I wouldn't want that. Are you certain I can't give you a ride?"

"Thank you, no."

He could hear the unspoken "Your Highness" in her tone, the polite curtsy buried within her words. His hands folded into fists. "I'll call you. If we can't see each other, you can at least take five minutes to talk."

She attempted a smile, but he caught the faint wobble and realized she wasn't anywhere near as in control as she'd like to pretend. He took a step in her direction intent on breaking through the vestiges of that control, but she flung up a hand, stopping him at the last second.

"Don't." Her voice broke on the word. She shot a swift, hunted glance toward the door. "Please let me go."

It wasn't what either of them wanted. He could change her mind with a single touch, but he didn't have the heart to stop her, to hurt her any more than she was already hurting. "I'll call you later," he repeated, more forcefully this time, and stepped aside.

She broke for the door, snatching up her purse as she went. He didn't waste any time. Dressing as swiftly as she, he made a beeline for the elevator. Juliana was already gone, but had sent the elevator back up for him. He shook his head as he stepped inside and stabbed the button for the garage.

He found her fascinating. Passionate. Kind. Wary. Like a wild creature in need of help, but fearful of becoming trapped. He could sympathize. Soon she'd discover they were both trapped in a situation not of their making, one with only a single solution. He fingered the ring he'd taken from the museum. It weighed heavily in his pocket. It was time to end this nonsense once and for all, he decided. Time to spring the trap.

He commandeered the car from the previous night and started it with a roar. Pulling out of the garage, he turned onto the street fronting the apartment complex. To his surprise, a crowd had gathered there. He glanced over as he passed, and what he saw had him slamming on his brakes and screeching to a halt.

Damn it to hell! Someone had sprung the trap ahead of him.

The elevator ride to the lobby seemed endless, stopping at every other floor. She'd been a fool to get involved with Lander. She'd known it from the start. At least with Stewart she could claim a certain level of naiveté. She'd been woefully inexperienced. Unfortunately, with Lander she could make no such claim. She'd committed the ultimate folly. She'd allowed herself to fall in love. To believe—if only for a moment—in fairy tales and happily-ever-after endings. It had been a mistake, one she'd never make again. She had no right to involve herself with a man who would be king. None.

The doors opened on to the lobby, and after returning the car to the penthouse, she walked briskly toward the exit, the rapid-fire chatter of her heels marking the speed of her passage. She never even looked up as she pushed through the doors leading outside, never saw them until she'd burst right into their midst.

"What's your name, miss?" The question was asked in Verdonian.

Flashbulbs exploded in her face and she flung up a hand to protect herself. "What…?"

Dozens of men and women hemmed her in on all sides, pressing, pressing, pressing. Microphones were shoved toward her, along with tape recorders and camera lenses. Everything took on a surreal quality. Noises grew too loud—the shrill, demanding voices, the desperate thrum of her heartbeat, the labored sound of her breathing. Odd, unwanted sensations heightened—the harsh feel of the sunlight scouring her face, leaving it naked and vulnerable to prying eyes. The stab of heat her panic induced, countered by the dank chill of fear. The stench of too many perfumed bodies, pulling, pulling, pulling.

"How long have you been seeing Prince Lander?" Verdonian again.

"What's he like in bed?" American. Female. City-slick and cynically amused. Followed by, "Who are you? You look familiar. You're not from Verdonia, are you, sweetie?"

Oh, God. Had she been recognized? "Please—"

"American," another crowed. "Definitely American."

She tried to push her way clear, but they weren't about to allow that. They reminded her of a pack of hyenas cornering a foolish gazelle who'd strayed too far from the herd. She was struck with a hideous sense of déjà vu. Another time, another place, but with the same rabid mob mentality, pushing, pushing, pushing.

"Did you know your father was already married?" the voices had shouted at the helpless eight-year-old she'd been back then. "How does it feel to be a bastard?"

The flashback to that hideous, long-ago moment only lasted an instant, but it was enough to cause her chest to tighten. "Please, move." She could feel the panic gnawing at the edges of her self-control and she fell back a pace only to be shoved stumbling into the center ring once again. "I don't know what you're talking about. I need to get to work."

"Where do you work?"

"Do you work for Prince Lander?"

"I wouldn't mind that sort of work." Laughter erupted at the American reporter's comment. "Hell, I'd be willing to pay for the pleasure, if it meant spending the better part of my day in bed with Prince Lander."

The laughter had cut off in the middle of the woman's comment, so the final words rang crude and unpleasant in the morning air. An uncomfortable silence descended, though Juliana remained too shocked and confused to judge the cause.

And then she heard him. He uttered just a single word, one that sang of salvation, even if it sounded more like a growl than a song. "Move."

As one, the reporters and paparazzi parted and Lander stood there looking as much like the Lion of Mt. Roche as she'd ever seen him. His hair swept back from his face like a mane, the sunlight picking out the streaks of blond among the tawny brown. Fierce green lights burned in his gaze, and every line of his face held an implicit promise of violence. He sliced through them with a jungle cat saunter, and took what belonged to him—her.

He caught her by the hand and she felt something slide onto her finger before he turned with her, facing the press. He eyed them one by one, his gaze lingering for a fraction of an instant on the American reporter.

"Remove her." Security closed in, security Juliana hadn't even noticed encircling the mob until then. "Escort her to the airport and see her on the first plane out of Verdonia." He cut off the woman's furious protests with a single glare. "No one treats my fiancée with such disrespect and continues working in this country." He lifted Juliana's hand to his mouth with old-fashioned gallantry and kissed it. "No one."

Every last person drew a collective breath, including Juliana. Before anyone could fire a single question, Lander draped an arm about her shoulders and whisked her through the crowd to his car. It sat in the middle of the street, the engine idling, the driver side door hanging ajar. He bundled her into the passenger seat before climbing behind the wheel. In the next instant they shot down the road, security cars clearing a path in front and behind.

"Are you okay?" Lander spared her a swift glance. "Damn it. You look like you're going to faint. Even your lips are white." He took his hand off the wheel long enough to stroke her cheek. "And your skin is like ice."

"It was… It was—" She drew in a deep, shuddering breath, striving to speak through chattering teeth. "I don't handle crowds like that very well."

"No one does. I'm sorry. I swore I'd protect you from that sort of media circus and I failed." A muscle jerked along his jawline. "I promise it won't happen again."

"Of course it will." It always did. Numb acceptance vied with a visceral fear. She twisted her hands together in silent agitation and suddenly realized she was wearing a ring. Glancing down, she gaped. It was Soul Mate, though she didn't have a clue how it had come to be on her finger. She thrust her hand beneath his nose, her fingers trembling so badly that red sparks exploded outward from the center of the amethyst. "What? How…?"

"I slipped it on your finger right before I announced our engagement."

For some reason, she couldn't get her brain to wrap around his explanation. "But we're not engaged."

He shot her a swift, humorous glance. "We are now."

Disjointed bits and pieces from her rescue coalesced into a less-than-cohesive whole. The *snap, snap, snap* of the reporters' jaws as they bit off pieces of her for public consumption. Her helplessness and fear. And then Lander had arrived, her knight in shining armor. And he'd said…he'd said, *No one treats my fiancée with such disrespect*….

She closed her eyes. That's right, she remembered that part. He'd called her his fiancée. He'd made that one reporter leave for being disrespectful. Then he'd lifted her hand and— She sucked air into her lungs and her eyes flashed open in shock. Her *left* hand. He'd lifted her left hand and kissed it, so that everyone would notice the ring he'd surreptitiously slipped onto her finger. She'd seen the astonished delight on the faces of the reporters. Had cringed from the speculation in their eyes as they'd scribbled their notes and recorded the moment for posterity with their cameras and video. She'd just been too far gone to comprehend the significance of what had happened.

"No!" She looked around with a rising sense of desperation. "Pull over. Pull the car over, right now. You don't realize what you've done. We have to go back and fix this before you're ruined. You have to tell the press we're not engaged. Please, Lander!"

He shot her another look, one of deepening concern. "Two more minutes and we'll be there. Hang on until then."

He was as good as his word. He spun into the winding drive that led to the palace and zipped up the road and through the gates at a rate of speed that spoke of long practice, and yet had her closing her eyes out of sheer panic. When they slowed, she peeked through her lashes in time to see him turn onto a small access road that circled toward the back of the palace.

"This way," he said as soon as they'd exited the car.

He led her through a warren of walkways and it was everything she could do to keep from battering him with a barrage of questions and demands—questions as to why he'd claimed they were engaged, and demands that they return to the apartment complex and tell the press the truth. A few minutes later they found themselves once again in a small, familiar glade at the path's end. In the center of the clearing stood the trellis gazebo she remembered so well, the structure barely visible beneath its canopy of white roses. Their heady perfume scented the air, stirring bittersweet memories of the last time she'd been here.

"Back to where it all began," she felt compelled to say.

"It didn't start here." He closed the distance between them. "It started in the ballroom when I looked up and saw you standing above me. I'd never seen anyone more beautiful than you."

"Love at first sight?" If only that were possible. "I already told you I don't believe in that. It's the stuff of fairy tales and fantasies and—" Her voice broke before she managed to harden it. "And make-believe."

"Don't." He gathered her close. "It'll all work out. I promise."

"How can it?" She pushed away from him. "You just don't get it. You think I'm Cinderella. But I'm not. I'm the ugly stepsister. You have to go back to the apartment. You have to tell all those reporters that you made a mistake. That you were just joking about our engagement."

"But I wasn't joking. And it's not a mistake." Even though she'd pulled free of his embrace, he didn't let her move beyond his reach. If she'd been the imaginative sort, she'd have suspected he was stalking her. "Besides, mistake or not, it's too late to take it back."

She stilled. "What do you mean?"

"By now the information is everywhere," he explained matter-of-factly. "Newspapers. Television. The Internet. All of the media outlets will be trumpeting the news. And every last one will be in the midst of a pitched battle to be the first to identify you."

She fought to draw air in her lungs. "Oh, God. You have no idea what you've done."

"What's wrong?" The sensation of being stalked intensified as he caged her against the gazebo. "Why are you in such a panic?"

Soft white roses kissed her face and shoulders while the vines snared her hair, delicately coaxing the curls loose from their confinement at the nape of her neck. "I warned you there were things you didn't know about me."

"Like what?"

Tears blinded her. *Say it! Just say the words.* "I'm illegitimate, Lander." There. It was in the open now. She'd claimed the awful truth. Even after all these years it still had the power to wound, stirring some of the most traumatic memories of her life. "I was eight when I found out, in a manner not that different from what happened outside the apartment complex. It was…it was a big scandal at the time. My mother, my brother. We were crucified by the press."

"Easy, sweetheart. It's all right."

"No, it's not all right!"

She covered her face with her hands, struggling to contain the flood of emotions, with only limited success. It was time to get this over with, to tell him the truth and be done with it. Past time, if she were honest. She'd known this moment was coming but had been too much of a coward to face it any sooner because her desire for Lander had outweighed basic common sense. Now she had no other choice but to deal with the situation and put an end to their involvement, once and for all. Slowly she dropped her arms to her sides and stood before him like a prisoner facing a firing squad.

"No one in Verdonia knows my name yet. But that American reporter recognized me. Once she's had time to think about it, she'll remember where she's seen me." Pain underscored each word, despite her best attempts to keep her voice emotionless. "And she'll be angry because you made her leave the country. She'll want to get even. She'll put things in the paper. Or online. Or go on some hideous talk show and air all the sordid details."

"What sordid details?"

She forced herself to speak unemotionally, though it was one of the toughest things she'd ever done. "My name is Juliana Rose…Arnaud. I'm Joc's sister. Most people in the States know me as Ana Arnaud, rather than Juliana. When it gets out that I'm the illegitimate daughter of a crook, the sister of a man who amassed his fortune through—what the press regards as—questionable means, you'll be crucified."

Lander's hands tightened on her shoulders. "It doesn't matter who your father is, or your brother. I'll protect you."

"It's not me who needs protecting!" She drew a ragged breath, staring at him in disbelief. "You say none of this matters, but you're wrong. It does matter. Don't you understand what I've done? I've ruined your reputation. At the very least, I've cost you the election. No one in Verdonia will want their king married to a bast—"

He stopped her with his mouth, cutting off the word before it could be fully uttered. It was as though he refused to have the air they breathed sullied with such an ugly declaration. Every last thought in her head evaporated beneath the heat of his embrace. He took her to new heights with that kiss, reassuring her without words. Adored her. Gentled her. Loved her.

"I don't care," he said between kisses. "The circumstances of your birth aren't what matter to me."

"My illegitimacy should matter. Don't you understand—"

"Trust me, Juliana. I understand more than you know." He snatched another kiss while she puzzled over that. Reaching behind her, he removed the clip at the nape of her neck, and with a swift flick of his wrist, sent it spinning over the nearest hedge. "God, I've wanted to do that since the first time you wore your hair in that annoying knot."

Before she could utter a single protest, he sank his fingers deep into the loosened strands and tumbled it into a fiery halo around her face. In between swift, teasing kisses he stripped off her suit jacket and released the top three buttons of her blouse. The entire time he edged her closer to the gazebo until they scaled the half dozen stairs and stepped inside.

Shadows draped the interior, and the scent of roses hung more heavily in the confined space. Intent on putting some distance between them, Juliana retreated to the padded wrought-iron bench in the middle of the gazebo and attempted to do up her blouse. Before she could get more than a single button through its hole, Lander sat next to her and swung her legs across his lap. Removing her heels, he tossed them through the archway onto the verdant grass beyond.

"What are you doing?" she demanded.

"Making love to my fiancée."

She stared at him, wide-eyed. "Stop calling me that. It's not a real engagement and I'm not making love in the palace gardens where anyone could stumble across us."

He shrugged. "Okay, then we'll talk some more. Have you told me everything you need to?" He smiled at her with such tenderness that it nearly broke her heart. "Any more confessions, my scandalous wife-to-be?"

"Aren't you listening? I'm not your wife-to-be. You haven't asked and I haven't accepted. This is nothing to make light of, Your Highness. It's serious."

He sobered, the laughter dying from his eyes. "I promise I'm not making light of it. The circumstances of your birth don't make any difference to me, or to how I feel about you. Nor does your relationship to Joc. But it infuriates me that you've been made to feel ashamed of something beyond your control."

Dear God, she'd have to tell him all of it. It was the only way to get him to understand. "It isn't just the circumstance of my birth," she insisted. "There's something else. Something worse."

If she were going to get through this next part she needed every ounce of control she possessed. She fixed her gaze on where Lander had tossed her shoes, one sitting as neatly as if she'd placed it on the grass, the other facedown, its stiletto heel stabbing skyward like a finger of doom. She retreated into a math equation to help clear her mind, working it through step by step. She'd nearly finished when Lander spoke.

"Would you mind telling me what the *hell* you're doing?"

She blinked. "I'm sorry. What did you say?"

"I asked what you were doing. It's like…you went away. One minute you were here and—" he snapped his fingers just shy of her nose "—the next you were gone. This isn't the first time it's happened, either."

"Oh. That."

"Yes. That."

"I was solving a second-order-linear-difference equation."

"Second order linear—"

"Difference equation. With constant coefficients." A reluctant smile broke through. "It's a mathematical equation. It helps reduce stress."

"And you do that in your head?"

Her brow crinkled in a frown. "I'm not sure I always get the answer right, but that's not the purpose."

"Of course not," he muttered. "Damn, woman, you never cease to amaze me." He gestured for her to continue, bringing them back on point. "Okay, let's hear it. What's the other scandal in your background? I don't suppose it has anything to do with a certain man named Stewart?"

"I'm afraid so."

She started to lace her fingers together, but finding she still wore Soul Mate threw her off stride and she hesitated, not quite certain what to do with her hands. Lander settled the matter for her. He pulled her closer and twined her arms around his neck. It seemed easiest to submit rather than to protest. He'd release her soon enough—once he heard all she had to say.

Juliana rested her head on his shoulder. "I used to be an accountant," she began.

"Too bad you didn't tell me when we first met. I might have offered you a job working for me. Our chief executive accountant, Lauren DeVida, left when my father died." His voice rumbled deep and soothing against her ear. "I assume you worked for your brother as an accountant?"

"Before heading Arnaud's Angels, I was his CEA."

"See? I was right. You'd have been perfect as Lauren's replacement. I'd bet you'd find keeping track of our amethyst exchange far more interesting than Joc's wheeling and dealing." He twined a rope of curls around his finger and gave it a playful tug. "And I'm sure you'd be as devoted to me as Lauren was to my father."

"No, I wouldn't," she retorted. "Because I no longer mix business and pleasure."

"Ah. Cue Stewart's entrance into your life," Lander guessed.

Juliana nodded, her cheek rubbing against downy-soft Egyptian cotton. "And then came Stewart. It's not a pretty story."

"Let me guess. Stewart worked in Arnaud's corporate headquarters, and the instant he discovered you were Joc's little sister, he moved in." When she stared at him in astonishment, he shrugged. "It's an old story, sweetheart."

She grimaced. "Then I guess this next part won't surprise you, either. He decided to steal from Joc and use me to do it. I was so madly in love with him—" She offered Lander an apologetic look. "Or thought I was, that I didn't catch on to what he was doing until too late."

"I assume when it all came out, you were vilified right along beside him, despite being the innocent in the story?"

It took her a long moment before she could bring herself to speak. "Thank you for believing in me. Not many people did, because of who my father was."

"And your brother."

There was a harsh undercurrent to his voice that disturbed her. "Joc may have gotten his start skating a slippery line. But as soon as he found his footing, he made sure all his dealings were dead honest. It's become a point of honor with him. Unfortunately, the press has a long memory and a suspicious nature. They've never forgotten those early days."

"You're a loyal sister."

"I have reason to be. He's always done everything in his power to protect me." She returned to the issue at hand with painful deliberation. "As for my part in Stewart's scam… Though I didn't help him, at least not directly, I wasn't innocent, either. I made it easy for him to pull it off. I was careless with passwords which allowed him access to computer documents he shouldn't have seen. I also let slip information that I should have kept confidential."

"Did he embezzle money?"

"No, he was too slick to remove it directly from any of Joc's accounts. Instead, he used insider knowledge to line his own pockets. You see, Joc has hundreds of businesses under dozens of corporate umbrellas. Stewart was able to gain access to records on outstanding bids, and on proposed buyouts and sell-offs. He acquired client lists, employee records, profit-and-loss statements." She splayed her hands across Lander's shoulders. "Basically, he used his position for insider trading. In addition, he influenced clients, revealed bids to competitors. You name it. If he could profit from it, he did it."

"I assume you discovered what he was up to."

"Eventually. But not until it was too late to fix. The scandal broke within weeks of my figuring out what was going on. By then it couldn't be covered up."

"Your own brother fired you?"

"No, I quit. I couldn't let Joc take the fall for my error in judgment." She removed Lander's ring and held it out to him. "You do understand why you have to call off the engagement? Why you have to tell the media it was all a huge misunderstanding? Even though Joc corroborated my side of things, there's always been a suspicion that I was more involved than anyone could prove. Especially since my last name is Arnaud, a fact that only added to the taint of suspicion."

"What I see is a young and naive woman taken advantage of by an experienced scam artist. You aren't the first person to have that happen, and you sure as hell won't be the last." He took the ring as she'd expected he would, then stunned her by saying, "The engagement stands. And just so you know, in my world a marriage always follows an engagement. Always."

Her eyes widened. He couldn't be serious. A fake engagement was one thing. But marriage? "You can't—"

"Think about it, sweetheart. How would it look if five minutes after I announce our engagement, I claim it was all a mistake? They have photos of you wearing my mother's ring." He took her left hand in his and slid Soul Mate back into place. "I wouldn't have given this ring to someone without due consideration, and the people of Verdonia know that."

Her fingers trembled in his grasp. "If you don't put a stop to this, you'll lose the election."

"Then I'll lose the election," he retorted implacably. "Better that than my honor."

His tone warned that their discussion was at an end, something she recognized from a lifetime's experience dealing with Joc. She inclined her head in apparent agreement, but she couldn't bring herself to give voice to the lie. When he pulled her back into his embrace, she went willingly enough. But inside she wept for the loss to come.

She told Lander about her relationship to Joc, expecting him to release her from their impromptu engagement. To distance himself from her. It was one thing to maintain an arm's-length business dealing with someone, even a man suspected of amassing his fortune through dubious means; it was another to marry into the family. Once the people of Verdonia discovered she was Ana Arnaud, the stain on Lander's reputation would be irreparable. Which left her with only one choice.

If Lander's honor prevented him from breaking their engagement, she'd have to see to it personally.

Seven

"You can't do this, Ana."

"Yes, Joc, I can and I will." Juliana put the finishing touches on her makeup, then slipped a pair of plain pearl studs through the holes in her ears. "If Lander refuses to stop this insanity, I'll do it for him. The press conference stands."

"Maybe Montgomery doesn't want to end your relationship. Maybe he's in love with you. Maybe he used the situation to force you into an engagement you'd never have considered otherwise. Have you thought of that?" Joc paced from one end of the bedroom to the other, before pausing behind her. "Well? Have you?"

It took her an instant to control the wild surge of longing, the reckless hope that flared to life before she could tamp it down. "Doubtful. It's a question of honor, not love."

Joc seized her by the shoulders and spun her around. "Why do you say that? Do you consider yourself unlovable?"

"Stop it, Joc." She wriggled free of his hold. "This isn't about love, and you know it. Lander feels responsible. He pursued me after I tried to end things between us, pushed us into an affair—not that I required much pushing. It's only natural that when the press found out about us, he felt honor bound to act. He practically told me as much."

"Bull."

She drew herself up. "Excuse me?"

"You heard me. Do you think I'd be so easily trapped into a marriage I didn't want? Hell, no. Nor would Lander. He could have found some other solution if he'd wanted. A less extreme one than announcing your engagement." Joc planted his fists on his hips and lowered his head in thought. "Didn't you tell me Lander had his mother's ring on him."

"Right. It was in his pocket. So?"

"So…" Joc lifted his head and pinned her with a keen gaze. "So, what was it doing in his pocket?"

She stared blankly. "I…I don't know." How *had* it ended up there? She struggled to recall. "I handed it to him when we were at the museum. And I think he stuck it into his pocket instead of returning it to the display case."

"Wait a minute. Take me through this step-by-step. His mother's engagement ring was at a museum, the national one here in Mt. Roche?"

"Yes. He was showing me the crown jewels after hours last night."

Joc cocked an inquiring eyebrow. "Just showing? If

it was all just showing, how did the ring end up outside the case? There had to be a bit of touching going on for that to happen."

"Okay, fine," she responded defensively. "Maybe I was also trying on some of the pieces."

He grinned. "Montgomery let you wear the crown jewels of Verdonia?"

"He might have." Her cheeks warmed. "No big deal."

"Yes, it is a big deal. Have you any idea how much expense and effort that would take to secure the premises so you two could play?" Joc glanced at her finger, then frowned. "Speaking of your engagement ring. Where is it?"

"I sent it back."

"Damn it, Juliana!"

"That's enough, Joc. The subject isn't open for debate. In case you've forgotten, there's a pack of reporters gathering outside my apartment. It would look odd if I wore Lander's engagement ring to a press conference announcing the end of our engagement."

She turned her back on her brother and started to pull her hair into a sleek knot at the nape of her neck until a memory of Lander tossing her clip into the shrubbery intruded. She hesitated, combing her fingers through the strands and watching the curls riot around her face and shoulders. Maybe she'd leave her hair loose. Just this once.

Joc came to stand behind her. "Okay, I won't debate the matter with you or try and explain why you're the biggest idiot I ever met. But I'd think, at the very least, you'd be curious to know why Lander stuck that ring in his pocket instead of returning it to the display case. Admit it. Aren't you curious?"

"No, I'm not." She glared at her reflection. She was being ridiculous. The only reason she wanted to leave her hair loose was because Lander liked it that way. With ruthless intent, she scraped back every last curl, anchoring the weighty mass with a spare clip. "He could have been stealing the ring, I suppose."

"Very funny." Joc leaned in, whispering close to her ear, "Maybe he took it because he'd been planning to propose all along."

Hope flamed anew. Was it possible? It did explain his keeping the ring. The next instant pain subdued every last spark of hope. No, no, no. She didn't dare allow herself to think along those lines. She'd drive herself crazy wondering about the what-might-have-beens. What might have been if she didn't bear the Arnaud name. If she hadn't been illegitimate. If she hadn't fallen for a scam artist and ruined her reputation beyond repair. She shook her head, forcing herself to focus on her one and only goal—protecting Lander.

"I have to go." She turned to confront her brother. Stubborn determination had settled into the crevices of his face, warning he wouldn't easily give up the argument. She didn't understand it. Why was he pushing this? She released her breath in a sigh. "What do you want, Joc? I mean, really."

"I want you to stay away from the press for a few days. Allow the situation time to settle down."

"You mean, do nothing?" She couldn't believe he was suggesting such a thing. "You always taught me that whenever a problem arose, you had to deal with it right away, before it had a chance to escalate. That's what I'm doing. Besides, if I don't act now, Lander will be the one paying the consequences. There's not much more the press can do to me."

"You don't give your fiancé enough credit."

"My fiancé," she repeated. Her eyes narrowed. "What are you up to? I would have thought you'd do everything possible to help me straighten out this mess, instead of throwing up roadblocks to maintain the status quo."

"I just want you happy. And I think Lander will make you happy."

Her expression softened. "That's sweet, especially considering your earlier opinion." She raised on tiptoe and planted a kiss on his cheek. "Thank you for caring."

"You aren't going to listen to me though, are you?"

"I can't. There's too much at stake. An entire country at risk."

She checked the mirror a final time. She'd chosen to wear her most conservative dress, the unrelenting black of the raw silk relieved by a simple strand of pearls and matching earrings. She'd also kept her makeup to a minimum, just a hint of blush, a swipe of mascara and a touch of lip gloss. Satisfied, she collected her purse and turned to leave.

"Are you coming?" she asked her brother. "Or am I on my own?"

"I wouldn't miss this for the world. If you need me, I'll be right behind you."

Her mouth twisted wryly. "Lurking in the shadows?"

He lifted a shoulder. "I do my best work from there."

Juliana took the elevator to the lobby, struggling with nerves. It didn't help that each blinking number mocked her descent, as though marking her fall from grace. She dreaded the next fifteen minutes with a passion that left her shaking. She couldn't think of anything worse than facing a horde of frenzied reporters. But she'd do it. She didn't have any other choice.

The doors parted, opening like the gates to hell. "Here goes nothing," she murmured bleakly.

She walked steadily across the lobby. The media circus milled just beyond the double glass doors with two uniformed apartment security guards all that kept them from storming the building. Sparing her brother a hunted look, she forced herself to push open the doors. Just as she stepped outside, she felt something tug at the back of her head, and the next instant her hair sprang free. Damn it! Somehow she'd lost her clip, not that she could do anything about it now.

A stray breeze kicked up as she stepped onto the landing outside the doorway, and fiery curls rioted about her face and shoulders. She shoved at the windswept barrage, then gave it up as a lost cause. Forcing herself to move forward, she paused at the head of the steps that led down into the sea of journalists. More than just journalists, she realized with a start. People from all walks of life swelled the press corps ranks. How had they known she'd be here, giving a press conference? Someone must have tipped them off.

A late-afternoon sun spotlighted her, shining into her eyes, which proved a blessing in disguise since it made it impossible to pick out individual faces. Questions pelted her from the moment she appeared, so many she couldn't single out one from another. She lifted a hand, and the clamor died to an unnerving silence, giving her an opportunity to speak.

"Thank you all for coming." She hesitated at the top of the steps, relieved to have at least that much space between her and the seething mob. Since her voice carried well from her position, she elected to remain where she was. "I'd like to make a statement, after which I will not be taking any questions."

Steady. She could do this. She had to; there was no other choice. "I'm here to announce that I'm formally breaking my engagement to Prince Lander. I'd like to assure all of you that I am both honored and flattered by His Highness's proposal and I wish—" To her horror her voice broke and it took her a heartbeat to gather up her control once again. She felt Joc edge closer and signaled him that she was okay and to stay back. "And I wish circumstances could have been different. Unfortunately, I wasn't forthcoming about my background with Prince Lander. He had no idea of my true identity when he proposed, since I was using my first and middle name in an attempt to protect my anonymity."

She bowed her head. "I was a fool. I should have told him the truth the moment we met, explained why any sort of serious relationship between us was out of the question." Looking up she offered a wistful smile, one that trembled around the edges. "Maybe some of you can understand how I felt. I wanted—just for a few hours—to believe in the fairy tale. To believe that I could find true love and live happily ever after. It was selfish and rash of me, not to mention unfair to Prince Lander. And for that I apologize to him, to you and to the people of Verdonia. I should have refused Prince Lander's proposal right from the start. Because I didn't, because I was self-indulgent, he's in this mess and it's all my fault."

"You still haven't told us your name," someone called from the middle of the pack of reporters.

No she hadn't. She drew a deep, calming breath and

stared over the heads of the crowd, into the setting sun. "It's Juliana Rose...Arnaud." She twisted her hands together and the absence of Soul Mate made her feel as though part of her had been cut away. "Most of you know me as Ana Arnaud."

All hell broke loose. The questions came fast and furious, one over top of another. She held up her hands. "Please. There's nothing left to be said. Be assured that Prince Lander had no idea who I was when he announced our engagement. This was all my fault, one I've now corrected. Thank you for coming."

She turned from the deafening shouts and escaped inside her apartment building, followed close behind by Joc. She'd done the right thing, even though it hurt more than she could have believed possible. The people of Verdonia needed Lander, a need far more urgent and vital than her own.

It was her fault they'd become engaged. Her fault that he felt honor bound to offer such an extreme solution to their predicament. And her fault that he stood to lose the election by insisting they marry. The only way he'd be the next king of Verdonia was if she released him from their engagement and ended their relationship. It struck her as the ultimate irony that his honor insisted he marry her, while hers insisted they part.

"It's better this way," she told her brother as they waited for the elevator.

"If this is better, then why are you crying?"

She lifted a hand to her cheek, surprised when her hand came away damp. How odd. She hadn't realized she'd been crying. "They're tears of joy for being out of this mess," she lied.

"It's interesting that your tears of joy look exactly the same as tears of misery. Why is that do you suppose?"

Her chin quivered. "When I figure it out, then we'll both know."

Lander faced the members of the press with calm determination. They all stood respectfully, waiting to hear what he had to say. No one shouted out comments or questions as they had with Juliana. The fact that they gave him the respect they refused to give her, annoyed the hell out of him. Not that he allowed his feelings to show.

"Thank you all for coming." He hesitated before admitting, "It would seem I'm in need of your help."

His opening statement was greeted with murmurs of surprise and a few encouraging smiles. So far, so good. "My fiancée, Juliana Arnaud, is under the mistaken impression that the people of Verdonia won't accept her as my wife. I'd like to see what we can do to change that."

"We?" one of the reporters asked.

"We Verdonians. You see, I believe she thinks her illegitimacy is an unacceptable stigma." Lander gave a what-can-you-do sort of shrug. "I've assured her on numerous occasions that this isn't true. That Verdonians judge people on their merits, not on their lineage. But she's having trouble accepting that fact. She feels that should we marry, it'll cost me the election."

Another of the reporters raised his hand and Lander pointed to him. "Your Highness, you referred to Ms. Arnaud as your fiancée. Are you saying the engagement *isn't* off?"

So, it was Ms. now, was it? That wasn't what they'd called her when they'd been shouting questions the night before. "As far as I'm concerned, it's not off. Ms.

Arnaud has a different opinion." Lander offered a smile that encouraged them to join him on his side of the dilemma—and once joined, to help. "I'd like to try and change her mind."

"I don't understand, Your Highness," a man in front spoke up. "What do you expect the Verdonian citizens to do?"

"First, I'd like to introduce all of you to the Juliana Arnaud *I* know. A woman who's kind and intelligent and compassionate, who puts honor before self-interest. If her press conference yesterday proved nothing else, it should have proved that she only wants the best for me and the people of this country." He leaned forward, speaking earnestly. "Juliana is a woman who, at the tender age of eight, discovered her father was a crook masquerading as a respected businessman. Imagine discovering not only that, but that your father had two families, one legitimate, the other not. And then imagine spending the next thirteen years branded with that illegitimacy and judged by it—hounded by some—despite the fact that you're the innocent byproduct of your parents' affair."

A woman in the middle of the pack raised her hand. "I don't see that the circumstances of your fiancée's birth have any importance. But other aspects of her background certainly do. According to my sources, she was suspected of helping her lover steal from her brother. That concerns me, as I'm sure it does most Verdonians. Any comment?"

He used silence to his advantage, waiting until it had stretched to the breaking point before responding. "First, Ms. Arnaud and the individual in question were never lovers." He paused to add impact to his statement.

"Secondly, she never helped this person, nor knew what he was up to until too late. She was thoroughly investigated and cleared by the authorities, but condemned by the jury of public opinion simply for being an Arnaud. The worst you can accuse her of was an unfortunate excess of naiveté. As soon as she discovered this man's duplicity, she reported him and resigned her position as a point of honor."

"Why is she in Verdonia?" questioned another reporter.

"I'm glad you asked." He'd hoped someone would. "She works for Arnaud's Angels, a charitable organization providing medical treatment to children in need. If you check, you'll discover that Verdonia has benefited greatly from the generosity of Angels, and that's largely thanks to Juliana."

"What do you hope to gain by this press conference, Your Highness?" came the final question.

He answered with absolute sincerity. "This is the woman I want to marry. I'm hoping the people of Verdonia can do what I've failed to do. Let Juliana know how you feel. Let her know that you'd welcome her as your princess." He held up Soul Mate, allowing the lights from the cameras to flicker off the brilliant amethyst. "I'd like all of you to help me put this ring back on her finger."

Juliana yanked the door open. The minute she saw who stood there, she started hyperventilating. "You… I…" She flapped her hand toward her living room where the television was replaying Lander's press conference for the umpteenth time that day. "What were you thinking?"

He strolled past her. "Oh, good. You're watching it."

She finally managed to wrap her tongue around the words clogging her brain. "Have you lost your mind?"

she demanded. "Have you any idea what you've done with that little performance you staged?"

He lifted an eyebrow in a regal fashion. "If you're going to speak to me like that, perhaps you should address me as Your Highness."

"You think I'm being rude? Too bad! I had it all fixed. I protected your honor. I fell on my damned sword for you." She pointed a shaking finger at the screen. "Why would you do…do *that* after all I went through to put an end to a bogus engagement?"

"Because I never considered it a bogus engagement, merely a premature one." He approached, and she realized she'd caged herself with a lion, a lion in deadly pursuit. He backed her against the edge of her couch and pinned her there. "I didn't want you to fall on your sword for me, Juliana. There was no need. I had everything under control."

He was too close, muddling her thoughts and rousing emotions she had no business feeling. Not anymore. "You consider that—" she gestured toward the television again "—under control?"

He tilted his head to one side. "What do you think is going to happen as a result of what I did?"

"I suspect everyone will erroneously believe we're engaged again."

A swift smile came and went. "Besides that."

"You'll lose the election," she stated flatly.

The fierceness of his frown had her catching her breath. She didn't know why, perhaps watching the respect and deference he'd garnered during his talk with the press had affected her in some strange way. But more than anytime since they'd first met, Lander struck her as every inch the royal. "I'm going to tell you this one final time, and then

I'll consider the topic closed. My relationship with you will not affect the outcome of this election. Are we clear?"

She nodded, wide-eyed.

"Topic finished?"

"Not quite," she dared to say. "I have one final question."

"One and only one." He folded his arms across his chest. "Ask."

"Why won't it affect the outcome?"

"Because within the next couple of weeks all of Verdonia will fall in love with you. I guarantee it. What you watched today is just the beginning."

She wanted to believe him. More than anything she hoped it was true. But she didn't dare. She'd spent too many years hardening herself against the callous stares and objectionable assumptions people made about her. That sort of thing didn't change overnight, not even by royal command. "How can you be so certain your people will accept me?" she asked.

His gaze held so much tenderness it brought tears to her eyes. "Because everything I said was true. You are kind and intelligent and compassionate. Most of all, you're honorable. As soon as the country sees that for themselves, they'll realize that not only do you belong here, but we need you."

She didn't know what to say to that, which was just as well since her throat had closed over. Taking her hand in his, he slipped Soul Mate back onto her finger. She started to stammer out a protest, one he stopped with a simple shake of his head.

"Don't refuse it. Not yet. Listen to me first."

"This is insane, Lander. We don't know each other all that well. It's happening too fast." The excuses flooded from her in a nervous rush, the one that concerned her the most, coming last. "You can't want to marry me."

"You're wrong. I do want to marry you. And I think you want to marry me, too." He gathered her up, fitting her into his embrace. They locked together as though they were missing puzzle pieces, finally made whole. His hand swept across her cheek in a light caress before his fingers forked into her curls and he tilted her face up to his. "There's no hurry, Juliana. We don't need to get married tomorrow or next week, or even next month. Wear the ring. If you decide our relationship is a mistake, you can always return it. In the meantime, we'll take it slow and easy."

She moistened her lips, afraid to believe. Afraid to trust or hope. Those qualities had been lost to her so long ago, she barely remembered possessing them. "Why don't we take it slow and easy, and then decide whether or not that ring belongs on my finger?"

He shook his head. "Everyone will be looking to see if you're wearing it. So, it's all or nothing, sweetheart. Right here and right now we either make a commitment or call it quits and go our separate ways. Your choice."

"But—"

"That's my offer. I refuse to go back and forth with the media playing 'is she or isn't she.'" He held her with a demanding gaze, his eyes an intense greenish gold. "Take a chance, Juliana. Trust me."

Oh, God. Trust. He would use that particular word. She leaned into him, closing her eyes against the urge to throw caution to the winds and give in to sweet temptation. "What happens if it doesn't work out?"

"You walk away, and I let you." She opened her eyes to discover the hard lines bracketing his mouth had softened. "I'm hoping you won't walk, because I'm not sure I can keep my side of that particular deal if you do."

His admission filled her with joy, a joy she forced herself to curb. She had another concern that might end everything before it ever began. "There's something else I need to know. Not about the election," she hastened to add.

"Why do I have the feeling I'm not going to like your next question?"

"Maybe because it has to do with Joc."

"Ah." His voice soured. "That might be it."

She caught her lip between her teeth. "You two don't like each other, do you?"

Lander shrugged. "We've had our differences."

"Then...what's he doing here in Verdonia? If you're not friends, why is he here?"

Lander's face lost all expression, filling her with apprehension. "I assume he came here to see you."

Not a chance. Joc adored her, she'd never doubted that. But he adored business more. If he'd come all this way, there was more drawing him to Verdonia than trying to talk her into resuming her old job at corporate headquarters. Her brother was a strong believer in the adage, "killing two birds with one stone." "Tell me, Lander. Do the two of you have some sort of business deal in the works?"

He shook his head. "You should ask your brother about that."

Her heart sank. "I'll take that as a yes. When he danced with me at the ball, he...he warned me about you. He warned me to stay away from you." She grimaced. "Now that I think about it, he pretty much warned me to stay away from you every time I saw him."

A smile of satisfaction eased the grimness from Lander's expression. "You didn't take his advice."

"No, I didn't." She gripped his arm, the amethyst on her ring glittering with red-blue fire. "I need you to tell me the truth. If we continue our relationship, will it hurt your business deal with him?"

He stared at her for an endless moment, his jaw tightening with growing tension. His eyes had darkened with some emotion she couldn't quite decipher, but it worried her. "Throwing yourself on your sword again?" When she stared at him in open dismay, he relented. "It hasn't and it won't."

Juliana couldn't disguise her relief. "You promise?"

"I promise."

His reply was so short and abrupt she wondered if she'd offended him again. But then he lowered his head and kissed her, putting an end to any further discussion, and she realized that he was far from offended. She tumbled back onto the couch with him and lost herself in his embrace. Somehow it would all work out. Somehow the people of Verdonia would accept her, maybe even love her. They had to.

Because she'd just realized that she was madly in love with their future king. And, though he hadn't said he loved her, too—the only dark cloud on the horizon— for the first time in years, she'd begun to trust again.

Lander flipped open his cell phone and placed a call. "It's done," he announced as soon as Joc answered.

"She's wearing your ring again?"

"That's what 'done' means, Arnaud," Lander snapped. He fought for control, fought even harder to keep his voice pitched low, though his intensity still came ripping through. "If your plan backfires, if she's hurt because of this, I will find a way to make you pay."

"You make sure she doesn't find out about our contract and she won't get hurt."

"This is wrong, Arnaud."

There was a momentary silence that Lander took for agreement. "I want her happy," Joc said gruffly. "For some reason, you make her happy. Since you're what she wants, you're what she gets. As for the contracts, they should be ready to sign by the end of the month. We don't sign until you two are married, so I suggest you keep things moving at your end."

Hell. "I promised her time."

"Take all the time you want…so long as it doesn't go past the end of the month. Juliana's not stupid. You take too long sealing the deal and she'll figure out what we're up to. Get her to the altar and fast."

Lander snapped the cell phone shut, wanting nothing more than to hurl it at the nearest wall. So much for honor. He didn't know who he was more disgusted with, Joc or himself. The only part in all this that brought him any pleasure was Juliana. He didn't know what to call what they had. Not love. He wasn't the type to allow his heart to rule his head. But he wanted her. He cared about her. And he looked forward to having her for his wife. Whatever that was, it would have to do.

He could only hope it would prove enough for Juliana.

Eight

"Your Highness, please." The dressmaker fluttered behind Lander as he entered the bedroom. "You can't be here. It's bad luck to see the bride in her wedding dress before the ceremony."

"Of course I can see her, Peri. My palace, my rules."

Across the room sheer pandemonium broke out. He grinned as Peri's assistants fell over each other to hold up lengths of fabric in an effort to hide Juliana from his view. From behind the makeshift barrier, he heard a crash, followed by a muffled oath, the sound of ripping silk and another louder curse. Then, "Damn it, Lander! What the hell are you doing here?"

He laughed, in part at the exasperation in his darling bride-to-be's voice and in part at the shocked expressions of the dressmaker and her assistants. "Why, I came to visit you, of course."

"I was with you not thirty minutes ago. You couldn't wait another thirty until I'm through here?"

"No, I can't." He settled cautiously onto a dainty davenport. When it proved sturdier than it appeared, he flung one leg over the armrest and settled back against the cushions. "The latest newspapers just arrived and I wanted to share them with you."

"I try and avoid newspapers whenever possible. I usually find them depressing, if not downright unpleasant."

He winced at the hint of vulnerability threaded through her comment. "These are neither depressing nor unpleasant. In fact, in the few days since our press conferences, they've all been rave reviews. For instance..." He selected a newspaper at random and turned to the appropriate page. "May I be the first to inform you, you are officially the cat's meow."

The assistants dropped the fabric they held, revealing a hand-painted dressing screen. Lander could see Juliana's silhouette on the far side as she was assisted in removing a billowing gown that one of the dressmakers whisked away for further alteration. Lord, she was gorgeous. All long, sweeping lines and soft, feminine curves. She poked her head around the side of the screen. In her haste to hide from him, her carefully knotted hair had become delightfully unknotted. For some reason, he found those bountiful curls fascinating.

"The cat's meow?" Her eyebrow winged upward. "Should I assume you're the cat?"

"You may so assume."

"Really?" She pretended to be disappointed. "I thought you were a lion."

"Cat. Lion." He shrugged. "If you don't like that nickname, how does Angel Ana grab you? It's the most popular of the dozen or so choices, although Angel seems a little much to me. And not terribly accurate, based on the words I just heard come out of that angelic mouth of yours."

Her eyes narrowed and he could see the warning flash of gold from clear across the room. "Would you please tell me what you're talking about?"

He held up a stack of newspapers. "I told you. I'm talking about these news articles."

She gripped the edge of the screen in alarm. "All those? They're all articles about me?" she asked in disbelief.

"Well, and me, too." His brows drew together. "At least, I think I'm in here somewhere. Probably listed in one of the footnotes as Angel Ana's bridegroom."

She started to come around the screen, only to be shoved back in place by one of Peri's assistants, who then bustled around the room, pretending not to listen as she straightened bolts of satin and tulle. "Are you trying to tell me that the press is saying nice things about me?" Disbelief underscored the question. "The press never has anything nice to say. You must have read it wrong."

"Did not." He riffled through the papers. "Here's one that's fairly illustrative. And I quote, 'Verdonia's princess-to-be, Angel Ana Arnaud, has the entire country at her feet. Standing before a crowd of reporters and local citizens, vibrant red hair tousled by the wind—'"

"Darn clip."

"'Angel Ana confirmed her engagement to Lucky Lander is back on—' Oh, there I'm mentioned. See? I'm also known as—damn, I hope Merrick and Miri don't read this, I'll never hear the end of it—Lander the Lovestruck, and Lovelorn Lander."

"They actually had the nerve to call you that?" Juliana asked faintly. "And the reporters are still breathing?"

"Breathing, just not functional. And you're interrupting. Let me read you the best part of the article. Where was I? Oh, yes. And I quote once again. 'All of Verdonia rallied in their efforts to encourage Ms. Arnaud to accept Prince Lander's offer of marriage. Now that she's once again wearing his ring, the entire country is celebrating the good news.' There, you see? Rave reviews."

"I don't understand." She sounded sincerely puzzled. "Usually all they want to print about me is scandal."

He tossed the papers aside and stood. "People are coming forward from all over Verdonia, sweetheart. All in support of you and full of reports of your many good deeds and kindnesses."

"You've helped so many of our children," one of the assistants offered.

"They even support you in Avernos," the dressmaker concurred. "As well they should."

Lander chuckled. "I'll bet that has von Folke's tail in a twist. What I wouldn't give to see that."

"Now, Your Highness," the dressmaker scolded, making shooing motions toward the door. "You need to go now so I can finish my job."

"Yes, yes. I'm leaving." Before anyone could stop him he crossed the room in a half-dozen swift strides. Yanking Juliana from behind the screen, he gave her a long, thorough kiss. "To hell with bad luck," he muttered against her mouth.

The instant he released her, Peri and her assistants ringed him, urging him toward the door. They almost succeeded in ousting him when he noticed piles of silk folded on top of her bed. "What are these?" he asked, detouring in that direction.

"Nightgowns. Please, Your Highness—"

He dug in his heels and gave the garments his full attention. "I'm not going anywhere until I see what you have here." He shook out each piece and studied it with an experienced eye. "I like this one. A definite yes for the green. This one's perfect. Great color. Please, God, yes. And—fair warning—" he swiveled toward Juliana and held up one of the selections "—if I ever see you in this, I rip it off and it goes directly into the fire."

"In that case, I'll be sure to wear it on our wedding night," she returned.

"Huh." He tilted his head to one side, considering. "Not a bad plan. Okay, fine. In another two weeks you can wear this one."

"Two weeks!" Juliana shot out from behind the screen again. "What are you talking about…two weeks?"

"Didn't I mention?" he asked with the utmost casualness. "We have an official wedding date."

"There must be some mistake," she began.

Returning the nightgowns to the bed, Lander cut her off. "Ladies? If you'll excuse us?" Without a word, the dressmaker and her assistants vanished from the room, leaving him alone with his bride-to-be. "Problem?"

Regarding him warily, Juliana snatched up her silk robe and belted it. "What happened to taking our time? To having a slow and easy engagement period?"

He approached and caught the ends of her belt. One hard tug sent her tumbling against him as the robe came undone. "We can wait, if that's what you'd prefer." He slid his arms inside her robe and around her waist. "I just felt the timing was good."

"Why? Why so soon?"

He shrugged. "It gives the country something to focus on other than my father's death. Instead of grieving, they have the opportunity to celebrate. It also pulls the focus off the amethyst crisis, giving me time to get to the bottom of the problem without worrying about media scrutiny."

"And the election?" She gave him a searching look. "Our marriage will help with that, too, won't it?"

"Now you're going to win the election for me?" He smiled in genuine amusement. "I seem to recall that just a few short days ago you were certain you would be responsible for my losing."

She shot him a teasing look, relaxing. "Hey, that was before I became the cat's meow. You marry me and the election's in the bag."

His amusement faded. "Tell me something, Juliana. Do you think I'd marry you…or not marry you, if it meant winning the election?"

She didn't hesitate. "No, of course not." She nibbled on her lower lip. "Do you really want to go through with this so quickly? You don't have any doubts at all?"

He found he could answer with absolute sincerity. "None."

She took a deep breath and then nodded, undisguised happiness giving her face a breathtaking radiance. "Then it looks like we have fourteen days in which to finish organizing a wedding. Maybe you'd better call Peri back in. We have a lot to do if we're going to be ready on time."

"Later." He took her mouth in a lingering kiss, one she returned with utter abandonment. "Much later."

When Lander finally left Juliana's room, he found

himself thinking that while his bride thought two weeks
far too soon for the ceremony, he found it an endless
wait. He groaned in frustration. He'd never make it.
Someone would slip up before then. Somehow she'd
find out about that ungodly bargain he'd made with Joc.
If the truth came out before the wedding could take
place, she would walk. Hell, she'd run. And Verdonia
would be ruined.

He shook his head in frustration. He should be
worried about putting his people first, about his country's economic future. Instead, all he could think about
was Juliana. If she found out the truth, it would be worse
than anything she'd experienced before. Being told in
such a harsh manner that she was illegitimate had been
bad. Having Stewart betray her trust and the public
scandal that had resulted from that betrayal, had been
worse. But this…this would destroy her. And it would
be all his fault.

A rolling drum of thunder woke Juliana on her
wedding day, while a white staccato blaze of lightning
greeted her the instant she opened her eyes. Rain
peppered the windows blown there by a gleeful wind that
rattled the sashes and shutters in a vain attempt to invade
her bedroom. Before she had an opportunity to do more
than groan in dismay, the lights flickered on overhead and
an entire platoon of determined women bustled in,
Lander's stepmother, Rachel, leading the parade.

"Perfect weather for a wedding," she announced.
"An excellent omen."

Juliana sat up in bed and drew her knees toward her
chest, eyeing the intruders with sleepy annoyance. They
were all Montgomery family members, the connections

so convoluted she needed a detailed genealogy to keep them straight. But it was tradition for them to help Juliana prepare for the wedding and keep her company, so she accepted their presence with good grace.

"A downpour on my wedding day is considered lucky?" A yawn interrupted the question.

"Without question." To a woman, the others gathered in the room nodded in agreement. "Rain on your wedding day means you'll be blessed with fertility and good fortune."

Juliana glanced dubiously toward the window. "And what does thunder and lightning mean?

"It signifies a very passionate love affair." Again the nods of agreement. Rachel came and sat on the edge of her bed. "Normally your mother would be performing the task I am today," she said, taking Juliána's hand in hers. "Lander told me she died when you were only ten. I hope you don't mind that I'm substituting for her."

Juliana shook her head. "Not at all. In fact, I appreciate it very much. It makes this part so much nicer."

Rachel brightened. "That's a relief." She tugged at Juliana's hand. "Up you go. You can't believe how much there is to do if we're to get you to the chapel on time."

The first item on Rachel's checklist was for Juliana to have breakfast with her and Lander's stepsister, Miri, so they could discuss the day's schedule. The two women were unmistakably mother and daughter, both with midnight-black hair as straight as Juliana's was curly. Both had the same unusual bottle-green eyes and flawless complexions, just as both were delightfully unreserved.

To Juliana's surprise, she sensed a certain strain between them and couldn't help but wonder if they'd just had an argument, or if the thread of discord she sensed indicated that they disapproved of the wedding. Juliana could understand if that were the cause. She'd only conversed with Rachel on a handful of occasions. And she'd never met Miri before. No doubt they questioned the speed with which the wedding was taking place.

She waited until they'd been served before tackling the issue with customary directness. "Do you disapprove of Lander and me marrying so quickly?"

Both woman glanced at her, startled. "No," they said in unison. It broke the tension and they all laughed.

Rachel leaned across the breakfast table and patted Juliana's arm. "You can't govern love. Or the speed with which it happens. Lander's father and I only knew each other a week before he proposed. Merrick met his bride no more than two before they wed. And yet, I've never seen a couple more in love." Juliana couldn't mistake the sincerity in the older woman's voice. "I'm delighted for you and Lander, and wish you only the best."

"Thank you." Relieved, she turned to Miri. "Lander speaks of you all the time. I'm sorry we haven't had an opportunity to meet before this. Have you been away?"

It was as though she'd hit them with a live wire. Both women jolted in shock and after exchanging one startled look, were careful to avoid the other's gaze. Juliana frowned. Oh, dear. If she didn't miss her guess, she'd just discovered the source of the strain she'd noticed earlier.

"My daughter has been enjoying a brief vacation," Rachel explained smoothly.

Miri's chin jerked upward in clear defiance and she tossed her waist-length hair back over her shoulder. "Actually, I was hiding out on the Caribbean island of Mazoné after helping Merrick abduct his wife."

"Miri!"

"Give it up, Mom. I'll bet Lander's already told her." She shot Juliana a challenging look. "Hasn't he?"

Juliana dabbed her mouth with the linen napkin. So much for asking what she'd assumed was an innocuous question. She'd opened up a veritable can of worms with that one casual inquiry. "He told me just the other day that Merrick had abducted Alyssa and that they ended up falling in love. But he didn't mention your part in the affair."

"I took Alyssa's place at the altar in order to give Merrick time to get away."

It was everything Juliana could do to keep her jaw from dropping open. She snatched up her teacup and buried her nose in her Earl Grey until she could control her expression. "Let me get this straight." She couldn't come up with a delicate way to phrase her question. "You're married to Prince Brandt, the man Lander will face in the upcoming election?"

"It's not legal." To Juliana's amusement, both women spoke in unison again.

"At least, we don't think it is," Miri added.

"What's he like?" Juliana asked, curious to know more about Lander's rival for the throne.

"He's tall, dark and handsome, of course."

"How can you call him handsome?" Rachel demanded. "He's too austere to be considered handsome."

"I don't agree. You just think that because his features are more severe than the Montgomerys', which sometimes makes him look hard." An odd quality crept into Miri's voice. "To answer your question, Juliana, he's self-contained yet passionate. And he has this old-world charm about him. He puts honor and duty and responsibility before everything else. Everything. And once he makes up his mind about something, he's impossible to sway."

"Interesting."

Juliana had learned to make swift assessments of people. Like her brother Joc, her judgment was rarely wrong—with the one disastrous exception of Stewart. Instinct told her Miri's feelings toward Brandt ran deep. Secrets burned in those spring-green eyes, as well as pain. Not wanting to add to her pain, Juliana deliberately changed the subject, addressing Rachel.

"So, what's next on my checklist?"

"After we've finished breakfast, you'll meet with Father Lonighan. He'll give you his formal blessing for the union and offer marital advice."

"Have fun with that."

"Miri! Then you have an hour to soak in your bath before the fun part begins." Rachel ticked off on her fingers. "A massage, facial, manicure and pedicure."

"Good Lord," Juliana murmured faintly.

"Then Miri and I will return to help with your hair and makeup."

Miri grinned. "What she means is, we'll watch while the experts take care of it. Then, in accordance to Verdonian tradition, Peri will sew you into your gown."

"Yes, she told me about that part," Juliana said. "But if I'm sewn in, how do I get out again, later?"

Rachel and Miri exchanged quick, mysterious smiles which worried Juliana no end. "You'll see," was all they'd say.

The rest of the day proceeded as outlined and the hours flew by. In no time she was having her hair fashioned into a gorgeous Gibson Girl hairstyle with ringlets framing her face and teasing the nape of her neck. Then the tiara she'd tried on at the museum was added to the arrangement. She hoped Lander would appreciate that she'd chosen something his mother had worn as a bride on a day very much like this one. She had the odd notion that it connected the two of them spiritually, one generation to another. As though aware of her feelings, Rachel gave her hand an understanding squeeze.

"Lander asked me to give this to you," she whispered, and offered Juliana a square jeweler's box.

Opening it, Juliana found the most striking pair of earrings she'd ever seen nestled inside on a velvet bed. They were a teardrop confection of diamonds and amethysts, both Royals and Blushes. Her hands trembled so badly she could barely put them on.

And finally came the gown itself, with Peri sewing her into it. As soon as she'd finished, she stepped back and nodded in a combination of approval and pride. The fitted bodice glittered with tiny amethysts of every shade. Layer after layer of tulle swept out from the narrow waistline in an endless train behind Juliana that folded and hooked to form an elegant bustle to make for easier maneuvering both before and after the actual ceremony.

And then they brought out her veil. A glorious confection of lace and tulle, it, too, glittered with amethysts. The lace and gemstones had all been set in an intricate pattern of swirls that managed to obscure her features while still allowing her to see. Now she understood how Miri had managed to fool Brandt when taking Alyssa's place at the altar.

As soon as Rachel twitched the veil into place, Juliana was escorted from her bedroom suite to the front of the palace where a flower-bedecked horse-drawn carriage awaited. Joc stood beside it wearing a dove-gray tux and looking more handsome than she'd ever seen him.

At some point the storm had passed, leaving the air scrubbed clean of humidity and filled with the delicious scent of early summer. A soft mist rose around the carriage, giving everything a fairy-tale quality. They rode through streets lined with Verdonians who cheered her passage. In no time they arrived at the chapel and Joc literally lifted her from the carriage and swung her to the flagstone entranceway.

"You know I only want the best for you," he said gruffly.

"Of course I know that."

"I'd hug you, but you're all—" He gestured to indicate her veil and dress. "I don't think I can wade through all that and back out again without getting it messed up."

She smiled, though she doubted he could see it through the veil. "I appreciate your restraint."

He offered his arm. "You ready?"

She took the question seriously. Was she ready? There were certain aspects of her future life with Lander that worried her, mainly living as a public figure. She'd spent a lifetime fighting the negative labels affixed to her name. How long would it take before she went from acclaimed to infamous again? It could happen. Public favor was a fickle thing.

And then she thought of Lander and how she felt about him. How much richer her life had become now that he was a part of it, and nothing else mattered. Nothing. "I'm ready," she said, and slipped her hand into the crook of Joc's arm.

Music drifted from the dim interior, Handel's "Minuet." They paused in the foyer where attendants straightened Juliana's gown and unhooked the train, spreading it behind her. "His Highness said he cut these himself," one of the women whispered, handing her a bouquet of fragrant white roses. "He said you'd know where they came from."

The gazebo. Tears sprang to Juliana's eyes and she started to lift the heavy blossoms to her nose, but the veil prevented her. As though realizing she was on the verge of ripping through the layers of lace and tulle, Joc urged her toward the sanctuary. The rippling majesty of horns broke into Stanley's "Trumpet Voluntary" the minute she appeared.

And that's when she saw Lander. He stood at attention waiting for her, dressed in full military whites, including a chest rippling with medals and an ornate saber belted at his hip—the Lion of Mt. Roche at his most majestic. Late-afternoon sunlight struck the stained glass windows on the west side of the chapel. The colors shattered, forming a rainbow of hues leading from where she stood to where she most wanted to be.

And then she was walking toward him. No, not walking. Floating, as though in a dream. The wedding service began, vanishing into the mists of memory almost as soon as it occurred. She vaguely recalled Joc joining her hand with Lander's. Father Lonighan spoke at length, his deep voice rumbling over her. Through it all, her full attention remained on the man professing to love, honor and cherish her, to protect her from all harm.

One of the clearest moments of the ceremony, a shard so piercing in intensity that it would forever remain a part of her, was when he slipped a pair of rings on her finger. The first was a heavy band of gold studded with Verdonia Royal amethysts. The second had her catching her breath. Instead of Soul Mate, he slid a far different ring on her finger, a delicate confection of diamonds and amethysts in a trio of unusual shades that complemented the earrings he'd given her earlier.

"I had it designed just for you," he murmured so only she could hear.

"Does it mean something?"

"Of course." His hazel eyes glowed with tenderness. "We'll see how long it takes you to figure out."

There wasn't further opportunity to speak. Father Lonighan gave them a final blessing, and the ceremony concluded with their being declared husband and wife. As tradition dictated, Lander had waited until the very end to lift her veil.

"I've never seen you look more beautiful," he told her.

Cupping her face, he took her mouth in the sweetest kiss they'd ever shared. Her eyes drifted closed as she lost herself in his embrace. The only thing that would have made the moment more perfect would have been if he'd told her he loved her. Just as the kiss ended, trumpets flared to life in a triumphant recessional. Lander took her arm and escorted her down the aisle and then outside where a roar of cheers greeted their appearance. The sun dipped low on the horizon spreading a rosy glow across the city. With a laugh, Lander swept his bride into his arms. Her train caught the breeze and billowed around them as he carried her to their waiting carriage. And in that moment Juliana didn't think she'd ever been happier.

Nine

After the wedding, Lander hosted a dinner reception for close friends and relatives. Laughter flowed as easily as the sparkling wine, both bright and effervescent and full of good cheer. During those brief hours, Juliana knew what Cinderella must have experienced after she'd married her prince. A rightness. A completion. For the first time in her life, Juliana felt loved and cherished. She felt like a real princess.

Toasts followed the dinner, some funny, some poignant, others heartwarming. Just as the last glass was raised, the majordomo appeared, inviting the guests to adjourn to the balcony to watch the fireworks display celebrating the royal marriage. When Juliana would have followed, Lander caught her hand and urged her in the opposite direction.

"We'll watch them from a more private location," he told her.

She didn't need any further encouragement. Gathering up the voluminous skirts of her wedding dress, she raced with him through the deserted corridors. At least, they appeared deserted. If security was stationed between the dining hall and Lander's private wing of the palace, they remained well hidden.

The two of them arrived at his bedroom suite breathless with laughter. She couldn't say what they'd found so amusing. Perhaps it was just their happiness bubbling over like uncorked champagne. Or maybe it was being alone together at last, the joyful anticipation of the hours to come. Pushing open the door, Lander swept Juliana into his arms and carried her across the threshold.

When he set her on her feet, she glanced around, her breath catching in her throat. Candles lit the room, dozens upon dozens of them on every surface, encircling them in a soft, warm glow. White rose petals were strewn across the carpet, providing a romantic pathway from door to bed. More of the petals were scattered on the satin sheets, their fragrance filling the room. Soft music issued from hidden speakers, and she paused to listen for a moment. It sounded so familiar. And then she realized why. The songs were selections from their wedding service.

"You did this, didn't you?" she asked in a broken voice.

"I'm forced to admit, I didn't light the candles. But, the rest…" He nodded. "I wanted it to be special for you."

"Thank you."

In the distance she heard a faint boom signaling the start of the fireworks, and she crossed to a set of French doors that opened onto the balcony. Lander joined her there, coming up behind and wrapping his arms around her waist, enfolding her in the warmth of his presence.

They watched the initial fireworks in silence, a blaze of color and explosion of sound that celebrated their union.

Gently he turned her. "Come. Let's get you out of that gown."

"I'm sewn into it, you know. I'm told it's traditional." Did he hear the sudden nervousness in her chatter? But then, how could he miss it? "No one's explained the origins to me."

"I believe it's to ensure the safe passage of the bride from her family's loving arms to that of her husband. Proof that no one has touched her during the interim."

"I've got news for you. There's plenty of touching that can go on without the bride removing her dress."

"Not if it's done right."

Juliana's mouth twitched. "Good point." She lifted an eyebrow. "So how do you propose to release me?"

"Like all good Verdonian husbands, I come prepared." He picked up a jeweled dagger resting on the bedside table. "This is called a *koffru*."

"I'm almost afraid to ask."

"You should be. It's a bride cutter."

"Lovely," she said dryly. "You're going to cut me with that thing?"

He responded to her jibe with a grin. Pulling her close, he spun her around so her back was to him. "It's not you I plan to cut. It's your gown."

"Don't ruin it!"

"Trust me, wife."

After sweeping her veil to one side, he sliced through the seam holding the back of her gown together with delicate precision. Inch by inch the knife skimmed down her spine until he reached her waist. And then it dove lower still, to a point just past her hips. Finished, he slid the dress from her body as well as the layered petticoat beneath. Offering her his hand, he helped her step free of the yards of satin and tulle. She stood before him, oddly self-conscious considering that they'd already been lovers, her only covering a few flimsy scraps of lace, her stockings, heels and garter, and her amethyst-studded veil and tiara.

"So beautiful," he murmured as he unhooked the veil and set it aside. When she would have removed the tiara, he stopped her. "My job." He slid the tiara from her hair, freeing the few curls that insisted on clinging to the jeweled hairpiece. "I wondered if you'd choose to wear this." His voice deepened. "It's in honor of my mother, isn't it?"

"Yes." Tension gripped his jaw, while sorrow cut brackets on either side of his mouth. Seeing him like that nearly broke her heart. "I wanted her to be a part of the ceremony in some small way."

"Thank you for that. She would have appreciated the gesture." He placed the tiara out of harm's way before turning back to her. "And now my favorite part."

One by one Lander removed the pins restraining her hair, catching the loosened pool of curls in his palms. Behind her fireworks lit up the night sky, flinging brilliant flashes of color across the hard, masculine planes of his face. Rich, vibrant sparks of green glowed in eyes filled with unmistakable hunger.

She reached for him with trembling hands, fervent and unabashed, fumbling with buttons and zips as she helped him remove his clothing. If she lingered over the corded muscles she found beneath his dress whites, he didn't complain, though she could feel the tension gathering across his shoulders. Nor did he complain when she followed the plunging vee of crisp, masculine hair that darted from chest to abdomen and farther still. She followed that line until she found the heart of his passion. She cupped him, stroked him, playing along the full length and breadth of him. It made her keenly aware of her own femininity and of his unrelenting maleness.

He took her mouth with a groan, plying her with fierce, desperate kisses. Her few remaining garments were a barrier swiftly eliminated and then it was her turn to be filled with an unnerving urgency, one painful in its intensity. He stroked her, the sensations growing hotter, headier, more concentrated. Just when her legs were on the point of giving out, he lifted her in his arms and carried her to the bed.

She drank in the aroma of the roses surrounding her, felt their silken caresses against her bare skin. But they were overlaid by another aroma and another caress, a more elemental, pervasively masculine one. He braced himself above her, touching, barely touching. Sliding with excruciating slowness. Rousing sensations that had her fevered one moment and chilled the next.

"Please, Lander. Now," she urged. "Make love to me now."

He didn't need a second invitation. He lowered himself to her, crushing the rose petals against her skin in an explosion of scent. Palming her thighs, he parted her legs, releasing his breath in a rough sigh as she welcomed him home. He surged into the liquid warmth, sealing their wedding vows as he sheathed himself fully within her.

"My bride," he whispered. "My princess. My wife."

He moved then, taking her with the utmost tenderness and care. Stroke built upon stroke, gathering the heat, driving it toward a burning need, escalating toward a frenzied desperation that left her utterly exposed, utterly abandoned to this most intimate of embraces. Her muscles tensed in anticipation of the ultimate surrender. When it came it stormed through them, demolishing every defense in an explosive release, one echoed by a final barrage of fireworks.

And in that moment of shattered completion, they became husband and wife in body, as well as name.

"Damn it, Joc. Could we get this over with?" Lander growled. "Juliana will wake any minute now. Considering it's our first day of marriage, I'd like her to do it in my arms, rather than waking to a cold bed."

"The final contracts are right here. All we have to do is get these lawyers to agree on the remaining two points and we're done. A few months from now, new business will flow into Verdonia, and hot damn—" he rubbed his hands together "—you've got a source of revenue to fill in the gaps left from the declining amethyst trade."

Lander grimaced. "It can't be soon enough. The Royals are becoming scarcer by the day. If something's not put in place to augment that lost income—and soon—it's going to have a disastrous effect on our economic stability. Nine months, a year from now, we're going to be hurting."

"We'd have an easier time finalizing our plans if you had an executive accountant working with us. What happened to yours?"

"She left after my father's funeral."

"Any chance she'd be willing to come in and lend a hand?"

"None. Lauren made that clear before she left. She

took my father's death pretty hard. I guess she'd been with him since—" Lander shook his head "—must have been before the death of my own mother. I believe she's somewhere in Spain enjoying an early retirement."

"I'm tempted to call Ana in and have her go through everything."

"Not a chance in hell."

Joc waved him silent. "I know. I know. It was just a thought."

"A bad one. We'll cope using our current accountants, not to mention the team of lawyers we both seem to have in excess." He shot a fulminating glare in the direction of the conference table. "Will they never finish?"

A light knock sounded at the door. Before Lander even saw the tumble of auburn curls and the gold-spiced eyes, he knew who it would be. Sure enough, Juliana poked her head around the door. She was dressed in a simple off-white silk shell and billowing skirt that had him remembering how beautiful she'd looked in her wedding gown. Even though her face was bare of makeup, she'd taken the time to put on the earrings he'd given her as a wedding present. It took every ounce of his self-possession to keep him from sweeping her into his arms and carrying her back to their bedroom.

"Oh, there you are." Relief brightened her face. "I thought I'd lost you."

"Not a chance." Lander pulled her into his arms, not giving a damn who was watching, and kissed her. "Good morning, wife. I'm sorry I wasn't there when you woke up," he said, and meant it.

"What's going on?" She glanced at her brother. "Hey, Joc. What are you doing here?"

"Business," he replied easily. "Just moving some of

my interests over here. You know me. Spread the wealth around."

"Right." She smiled at her brother. "Lander wouldn't discuss it, but I had a feeling you two were in negotiations over some deal or another."

"Oh, we're long past the negotiation stage. We should be done within the hour."

"Why did you have to wait until this morning to finalize everything?" To Lander's amusement, she shifted into scold mode. "In case you didn't realize, your timing stinks, Joc. That's not like you. You usually have impeccable timing."

"Sorry, Ana." Joc worked to appear suitably chastised. "I guess your wedding threw it off. If it makes you feel any better, we're at the sign, seal and delivery stage. As soon as that's done, you two lovebirds can take off on your honeymoon."

Juliana laughed, slanting a mischievous glance up at Lander. "I've worked with Joc on countless contracts. I know all about the delivery stage. One of the first things my brother taught me was to always wait until every last precontractual condition has been met before signing any agreement. He drummed the importance of it into me during every negotiation." She lowered her voice in a mocking imitation of Joc's Texan drawl. "Don't sign based on promises, Ana. Wait until they've done what they said they'd do before putting your name on the dotted line. It's all about leverage. It's all about getting what you paid for." Her gaze flashed from husband to brother. "So, what's left to do? Anything I can help with?"

"No!" Joc and Lander replied in unison, far too emphatically.

Juliana froze, and the tiniest of clouds drifted across

her expression. The silence thinned. Sharpened. Became painfully acute.

"Your Highness?" One of Lander's team of lawyers rose. "Excuse me, sir, but we can't move to the next stage until Mr. Arnaud has signed the papers indicating that you've fulfilled all the preconditions to the contract."

Juliana stiffened and the clouds from earlier deepened, piling darkly across her face and dimming the brilliance of her eyes. She untangled herself from Lander's embrace and took a quick step in her brother's direction. "What conditions are they talking about? What did Lander have to do in order to get your business?"

"It's not important," Joc dismissed the question. "Details. Nothing for you to worry about."

One look warned Lander she wasn't buying her brother's glib reply. He signaled the lawyers, jerking his head toward the door. "Out."

They didn't wait for a second invitation. Within thirty seconds they'd cleared the room. The minute the door closed behind them, Juliana spoke again, her analytical brain focused to a pinprick. "Joc, did you ever refuse to do business with Lander because he and I were having an affair?"

Lander relaxed ever so slightly, as did Joc.

"No, Ana. I didn't."

She spared Lander a swift, wary glance that had him freezing up again. "Maybe…maybe all this time I had it backward," she murmured. "Let's try it from this direction. Did you ever refuse to do business with Lander unless he and I became involved? No, you wouldn't have done that. You wouldn't have settled for anything less than—" She broke off, wide-eyed.

"Ana—"

She stumbled backward toward the door. "Oh, no. Tell me you didn't do that. Tell me *that* isn't one of the conditions of your contract."

Lander took a step in her direction. "Honey—"

She held up a hand. "I'm so stupid. How could I still be so naive after Stewart?" She shook her head, curls frothing around her face. Her complexion had turned as pale as her ensemble, stretched fragile and translucent across her elegant bone structure. Her heart fluttered at the base of her throat like the wings of a wild bird fighting the bars of her cage. "One plus one always equals two. Always. You'd think I'd remember that."

Joc frowned in confusion, but Lander instantly understood. He wished he could deny the conclusions she'd reached, but how could he when she was all too right? He'd never before seen such a look of devastation on a woman's face. The fact that that woman was his wife nearly destroyed him.

"Am I actually written into the contract, Joc?" she asked with amazing composure. "Section C, Subparagraph Four, Line Sixteen. In exchange for my basing X, Y and Z business in Verdonia you will marry my sister. If I read those contracts on the table over there, will I find my name in them?" When neither man twitched so much as a muscle, she swept relentlessly onward. "No? Not there? Then you must have decided my future over brandy and cigars. I'm a gentleman's handshake, aren't I? Marry my sister and I'll do this contract with you."

"Sweetheart, don't—"

Her composure shattered, her breath escaping in a sob. "Oh, God. You don't have to say another word. I get it. I do. My marriage is nothing more than a business deal." Her laugh was a painful splinter of sound. "Do I have all the details right? Have I missed anything?"

"Listen to me, Juliana," Lander began.

But she had no intention of listening. Before he'd even gotten the words out, she'd turned and made a beeline for the door. Flinging it open, she darted into the corridor. She heard Lander giving chase behind her. He caught up with her just as she burst into their bedroom suite.

Slamming the door closed behind them, he snagged her arm and spun her around. "Listen to me, damn it!"

"Listen to what?" She could hear the fury in her own voice and fought to modulate it, fought for a measure of restraint. Once upon a time, she might have succeeded. But this hurt went too deep to keep inside, the pain too raw to bottle up. "Whatever you have to say to me will either be a lie or an excuse. Which one were you planning on using?"

"Neither. I was planning on giving you the truth… and an explanation."

She cut him off with a swipe of her hand. "You don't need to explain. You did that weeks ago. I just wasn't paying close enough attention."

"I have no idea what you're talking about." He forked his fingers through his hair, the lion rumpling his mane. "What did I explain to you? Where? When?"

Her breath came far too quickly, her thoughts racing too fast for coherency. "We were in my office. Don't you remember? You were trying to convince me to continue our relationship after our one-night stand. And when I told you it wouldn't be in Verdonia's best interest, you said—" Her eyes fluttered closed as she strove to calm down enough to recollect his exact words. "You said your personal life has never interfered with your duty to your country, that duty takes primary importance over everything. Always."

Oh, God, why hadn't she listened? Why hadn't she understood? She'd been so caught up in the dream, in the fairy tale, that she'd forgotten what reality was all about. Well, she remembered now. It had come crashing down on her with a vengeance, destroying her from the inside out. "But I get it now, Lander. Marrying me meant that Verdonia would be protected from economic ruin. You didn't marry me because you loved me. You married me to protect Verdonia."

"You're right. You're absolutely right." Desperation had him pacing, and he ate up the length of the room with long, swift strides. "Joc came to me with his proposition. Said he had a sister he wanted me to marry."

"Me."

He swiveled to face her. "No, not you. Ana Arnaud." He closed in on her and she drew inward, flinching away from him. "I told him to go to hell. I told him I might have considered such an outrageous suggestion the week before, but not then. I'd met someone, I told him. Juliana Rose. But the joke was on me, wasn't it? Because when he showed me a picture of his sister, damned if Juliana Rose and Ana Arnaud weren't one and the same person. An interesting coincidence, don't you think?"

Her eyes narrowed. "Coincidence? You say that like you think—" Her breath escaped in a hiss and her control snapped. "You believe I was in on it?" she demanded, livid. "You think I plotted with Joc to force you to the altar?"

"The possibility occurred to me. You show up at the first ball we'd thrown since my father's death. You're using your first and middle name, conveniently omitting your last. Your brother arrives the same evening. We spend one unforgettable night together, and all of the sudden Joc is talking contracts and marriage."

She shook her head in disbelief, too full of anguish to speak, afraid she might break if she tried. If that happened, all her most private emotions would come spilling out in a hysterical flood. Once loosened from her control, she could no more call those emotions back than she could gather up a single raindrop out of a downpour.

Lander started toward her again. "So, yes. I admit it. I considered the possibility that you and Joc were setting me up. And you know what I decided?" He pursued her until he'd backed her against the bed. "I decided, who cares if that's how it went down? I wanted you. You wanted me. And then there was Verdonia to consider. With the amethyst mines played out, the country's on the verge of economic collapse. So, hell yes, Princess. I agreed to marry you. What would you have done?"

"I'd have told you the truth," she argued bitterly. "Given you a choice."

"Really?" He cocked an eyebrow, his expression skeptical. "Would you have agreed to marry me if I'd been upfront with you?"

She hesitated. Would she have? "I don't know," she conceded.

"At least you're honest about it." He lifted a shoulder in a weary shrug. "I suspected that might be your answer, and I couldn't afford to take the chance you might refuse my proposal. When the press found out about us—Joc's doing, I assume—I took advantage of the situation and had my ring on your finger before you had an opportunity to react."

"You put your country first, just as you warned you would."

He wanted to deny it, she could tell. "Yes. And let me be clear about something else, as long as we're being so damned honest. I'd do it all over again. The situation is too critical for me to leave anything to chance."

Resolution took hold, hard and implacable. "I can't live like that. I wish I could, but I can't." She looked around the room, seeking an avenue of escape. "I have to leave."

He reached for her. Fingers and curls seemed to find each other of their own accord, snaring and tangling. Clinging. Joining. "You're my wife."

"Bought and paid for." Her voice broke on the final words. Helpless tears gathered in her eyes. "That makes me property, not a wife. At least not a real one."

He snatched a kiss, then another. She remained helpless beneath the onslaught, her body softening, responding, betraying her need. "Stay," he demanded between kisses. "We'll find a way to work this out."

The tears fell then. Hopelessness drove them, a despair so deep and pervasive that nothing he said or did could make it right again. After Stewart, she'd thrown up a protective wall and hidden behind it, afraid to allow anyone access in case they hurt her again. Lander had pulled down that wall, brick by brick. He'd set those emotions free and she'd allowed it to happen, because she'd wanted—more than anything—to find love.

A coldness slipped through her veins, stealing the warmth his arms provided. She'd believed this man fulfilled her in every way possible, aligned her, balanced her. She'd thought she'd found her soul mate. And instead it had been an illusion. What he'd offered hadn't been real. What she'd hoped to find with him hadn't existed. Now all that remained was an empty shell.

She untangled herself from his embrace. He didn't want to release her any more than she wanted to go. Fingers and curls fought her, resisting, before being forced to part. No matter what it took, no matter how difficult, she had to walk away. She had to run. She wouldn't survive the pain if she didn't.

"I'm sorry, Lander. I can't stay." Her voice wobbled, not that there was any way to prevent it. "I'm going to ask Joc to take me back to the States while I consider my options. You two can decide how best to settle any outstanding contractual issues."

She started to remove her wedding rings and earrings, and he stopped her before the rings left her finger. "Keep them," he ordered.

Her gaze lifted to lock with his, a desperate, searching look. If only he'd say the words, just three simple words that would make all the difference in the world. But either he didn't know them, or he didn't feel for her what she felt for him. Time to concede defeat. It was over, the fairy tale ended before it had even begun. Without another word, she turned and left her husband.

Juliana was already on Joc's plane when her brother arrived. After shooting her a single look of concern, he gave his full attention to the pilot and attendants, issuing instructions in a low voice. He must have asked for privacy because they were immediately left alone in the spacious cabin.

"Ana, I'm so sorry." He came to sit on the armrest of the seat across the aisle from her. "I screwed up. I know that. But I swear I was acting in your best interests."

There had never been any question in her mind about that. Her brother had spent most of his life caring for her. Protecting her. Trying to provide everything she could ever want or need. But this…! "Why did you do it, Joc?" The blistering anger from earlier had gone, leaving behind a cold, bottomless fury. "How could forcing Lander to marry me possibly be in my best interests?"

"Because you deserved to be a princess." Determination filled his voice. "To be a queen, if that's what the people of Verdonia decide."

"How dare you!" she snapped. "What made you think I wanted to be a princess, let alone a queen?"

He stilled, taken aback. It had been a long time since anyone had ever questioned the rightness of his decisions, and having his little sister do it clearly left him unsettled. "Do you think I don't know how hideous the past seventeen years have been?" he tried to explain. "How you've suffered at the hands of the media? For a while I thought you'd come to terms with it. Put it behind you. You seemed to love your job." His expression darkened. "Until Stewart."

"And because of that you forced Lander to propose to me? To marry me? Was a contractual marriage supposed to protect me somehow? To ensure I live happily ever after?" Her mouth worked. "How could you do that to either Lander or me?"

"Don't you see? It's because I love you so much that I want what's best for you."

"You can't order the world and everyone in it to your convenience."

His jaw took on a stubborn set. "Why not?"

"Joc!"

He waved that aside. "Listen to me, Ana. There's something I haven't told you about my relationship with Montgomery. *I* owe *him*. That's why I came to Verdonia. That's why I agreed to help him."

Her brows pulled together. "What are you talking about?"

"We had a rather contentious relationship at Harvard." His mouth twisted. "I guess that would be a generous description considering how much I hated the man."

"You hated Lander? But, why?"

Joc's eyes were black with emotion. "You know why. Because he represented everything we weren't. He had the name, the heritage, the perfect life. He was the golden child. So I went after him to prove who was better. Grades, women, sports. You name it, I had to beat him. And in the end, I did. I graduated just ahead of him." He grimaced. "The bastard even had the nerve to shake my hand when he congratulated me."

Juliana shook her head. "I don't understand. How does that translate into your owing him?"

"His cronies decided that the only way I could have come out ahead of Montgomery was if I cheated. They beat the snot out of me, determined to get me to confess."

Understanding struck. "Lander rescued you, didn't he?"

"Yeah. I've never seen anything like it. He mowed through every last one of them and then carted me off to the hospital. I swore to him that day that if he ever needed anything, if it was in my power, I'd give it to him." His gaze fixed on her. "So, you see, he didn't have to marry you. If he'd refused, he knew damn well I would still have lived up to my part of our agreement.

There's only one reason he went along with my condition. He loves you. You have to believe that."

"But I'll never be one hundred percent certain," she shot back. "If someday he decides he does love me, I'll never know if it's what's actually in his heart or if it's part of his contract with you. I'll suspect every word he says. Every gesture he makes. Every gift he gives me. I'll never know. Not for sure."

Her brother stared at her in stunned horror. "No. That's…that's not right."

She bowed her head. "None of this is right." She pushed herself to her feet. She'd never felt so tired before, nor so defeated. "I'm going into the back to lie down. Please ask the attendants not to disturb me."

He caught her hand and squeezed it. "I'll watch out for you."

"You always do." She couldn't bring herself to look at him. "The problem is, I'm all grown up now. It's time I watched out for myself, even if it means falling down on occasion and skinning my knee. It's time to let go, Joc. You have your own life to live. Now let me live mine."

She didn't wait for his response. It didn't matter what Joc said or did anymore. Her declaration had been as much for her own benefit as it had been for her brother's. There had been the ring of truth to her words, a message from herself to herself. It was past time she took charge of her life. Long past time.

Ten

Juliana never did recall those first bleak days back in Dallas. They passed in a blur of pain and confusion, as well as a desperate, bone-deep despair. The minute she landed in Texas, she yearned to turn around and fly right back to her husband. But she couldn't. Not the way things stood between them. By the end of the first week, she knew she had to follow the advice she'd given herself on that last hideous morning in Verdonia. It was time to take charge of her life. There were decisions to make and a resignation to tender to her brother, something she intended to do that very day.

It didn't take long to drive into the city. Joc owned a full city block worth of office building in the heart of Dallas, a soaring glass and chrome structure that stabbed skyward in a gradually narrowing column. It was simply labeled Arnaud's. Security waved her through to Joc's private elevator, and upon exiting she found his personal assistant, Maggie, sitting in her usual spot outside his office.

The older woman looked up from her typing and smiled at Juliana over the top of her reading glasses. "Hey, there, girl. Or should I say, Your Highness?"

"You should not." Juliana cast a determined glance at the door leading to Joc's inner sanctum. "Is he around?"

"Can't you tell from the growls and snarls coming from in there?"

"That bad?"

"The worst I've seen him in a long time. Maybe you can snap him out of it."

"I'll see what I can do."

"His employees would be most grateful."

Taking a deep breath, Juliana entered Joc's office. She found him standing with his back to the door, staring out of the floor-to-ceiling windows at the Dallas skyline. "Damn it, I want some answers," he snapped as she slipped into the room. Realizing he was on speaker phone, she remained silent.

"You heard me." Juliana jumped in shock at the sound of her husband's voice. "I don't want her back in the country. I don't care what you have to do, just keep her with you in Dallas. Is that clear?"

"You don't give me orders, Montgomery."

"I do about this. I won't be changing my mind. If she tries to return, I swear I'll ban her from the damn country."

She must have made some small sound because Joc spun around. The words he uttered were some of the coarsest she'd ever heard him use. "Would you care to repeat that for your wife's benefit, Your Highness? She just walked into my office. Judging by her expression, I'd say she overheard every word you said."

An endless pause followed. Then the man she loved more than life itself replied, "If she heard, there's no point in my repeating it. I'll assume my message has been delivered and we can be done with this nonsense." He made the statement in a flat, emotionless voice, one so unlike his own, if she hadn't known it was her husband, she'd have thought she was listening to a stranger.

It took her three tries to answer him. "I'll have my wedding rings messengered to you first thing tomorrow."

"Don't bother. I don't want them back." And with that, the connection went dead.

Juliana stared blindly at her brother while she fought to breathe. "I…" She tried again. "I just came by to tender my resignation. If you'll excuse me—"

"Ana, wait." He started toward her. "There's something you don't know."

But she didn't wait. Turning, she walked steady as a rock from the office. Later, much later she'd break. But not here. And not now.

As Lander hung up the phone, he knew that he'd completely and utterly lost his wife—the one woman he'd ever truly loved.

Who'd have thought him capable of that particular emotion? How had that happened? When had it happened? Before their wedding, he knew that much. Certainly before he'd implemented the design for her wedding rings. Maybe it had happened the first time he'd seen her, when he'd mistaken love for lust. Leaning back in his chair, he closed his eyes, images of Juliana flashing through his mind.

His bride floating up the aisle toward him in that spectacular wedding gown and veil, her eyes gazing at him through layers of tulle, glowing a brilliant brown seasoned with gold. His wife, her skin more silken than the sheets she lay on, opening herself to him, crying his name as he brought her to completion. His princess, breaking their engagement in order to protect him, while facing down a pack of snarling reporters. She'd done all that for him. How could he do any less for her?

Even so, it hurt. A deep, immeasurable hurt. He'd thought his love for Verdonia outweighed everything. That he was incapable of the sort of love touted by poets and romantic fools. But that wasn't true. He was more than capable. It had hidden within, asleep until Juliana had come into his life. And what had he done with it when it had been gifted to him? He'd done everything in his power to destroy it.

"Excuse me, Your Highness." His majordomo stood in the open doorway to his office. "The Temporary Governing Council has requested your presence."

"Thank you, Timothy. Will you inform them that I'm on my way?"

"Yes, sire. Immediately." He hesitated. "Is there anything I can do to help?"

"There's nothing." Lander offered an encouraging smile. "Everything will be fine. I haven't done anything wrong, any more than my father did. The truth will come out."

"Yes, sir. Of course it will. No one doubts that for a minute."

Lander only wished that were true. Unfortunately, someone somewhere had pointed the finger in his direction, blaming the Montgomerys for the amethyst crisis. And he wasn't certain he could prove them wrong. The TGC, put in place to govern Verdonia until after the election, had no choice but to act on the allegations.

Added to that, news of Juliana's return to the States on the morning following their wedding had leaked almost as soon as she'd stepped onto Joc's plane. He'd anticipated the resulting public outcry and had been prepared to deal with it. But when news of the investigation had broken later that same afternoon, her disappearance had only added fuel to the fire of suspicion. Why would she have left the day after her wedding if she hadn't believed her husband guilty of wrongdoing? The fact that she'd flown out with her brother had only made the entire affair more suspect. Even the infamous Joc Arnaud had refused to stand by Prince Lander, the gossips had whispered.

The scandal threatened to rip his country apart. Until he could get it straightened out—*if* he could get it straightened out, he wanted Juliana well away from the media bloodbath.

The minute Juliana hit the street, she hailed a cab. "Drive," she instructed the cabbie as soon as he pulled curbside.

"Where do you want me to go?"

"Anywhere. In circles for all I care."

Sliding into the back, she began to shake, her hands trembling so badly the diamonds and amethysts on her rings flashed with urgent fire. She stared blindly at them as she fought for control, and when her cell phone rang, it was all she could do to answer it. She expected to hear her brother's voice. Instead her mother-in-law responded to her abrupt greeting.

"Have you heard?" Rachel asked without preamble. "About Lander?"

"I…I spoke to him ten minutes ago." If those few terse sentences could be considered speaking. "Has something happened to him?"

Rachel groaned. "He hasn't told you about the charges, has he?"

"Joc tried to tell me something when I left his office, but—" As her mother-in-law's comment sank in, she straightened in her seat. "What's wrong, Rachel? What charges are you talking about?"

"He and his father are accused of…misappropriation, I guess is the most tactful word."

Misappropriation? Did she mean…*theft?* "Did I hear you right? Lander's been accused of embezzling money?"

"Amethysts. He's been charged with skimming a portion of the outflow and selling the gems on the black market. Apparently, there's conclusive documentation to back up the accusation."

"That's a crock, and you know it," Juliana declared irately. She thrust a hand through her hair, sending curls flying. "Lander would never do anything so dishonorable. Nor would he be party to anything that would harm Verdonia."

There was an instant of silence, then Rachel whispered, "Thank you, Juliana. I was so afraid you left because you believed he was guilty."

"I left because I found out he didn't love me," she responded without thought.

"No! Whatever gave you that idea?" There was a momentary pause and then Rachel continued. "Never mind. That's none of my business." She hastened to change the subject. "Your brother told me you were the best there is when it comes to accounting and finance. Would you be willing to examine the records and see if there's something our people have missed?"

Juliana didn't hesitate. "I'll be there as soon as I can." Of course, returning to Verdonia meant facing Lander again, something she wasn't prepared to do. Not after their phone conversation. "There's one condition."

"Name it."

"I don't want Lander to know I'm in Verdonia."

"Oh. I…I guess I can do that. At least, I can promise I won't tell him. I can't promise that he won't find out from some other source. Will that be acceptable?" When Juliana reluctantly agreed, Rachel added, "Tell me, my dear. Did you ever figure out what your wedding rings meant?" Without waiting for an answer, she hung up.

Juliana flipped her cell phone shut, and after a momentary hesitation, held out her hand. She stared at the rings curiously. They were such a beautiful set. Her mouth curved upward in a wistful smile as she remembered the moment when Lander had slid the band and engagement ring onto her finger. She recalled that he'd said the design meant something, as well. Something she was supposed to figure out. With everything that had happened in the interim, she'd forgotten until Rachel's reminder. Now she looked, really looked at the pair.

The wedding band itself was set with an unbroken circle of Verdonia Royal amethysts. Royals, for soul mates. Hah. As if. But the engagement ring, was another matter. On the outer portion of either side were a scattering of tiny Blushes set in gold filigree. Farther inward the amethysts grew progressively larger and changed in color to a shade she'd never seen before, becoming mixed with diamonds until the very middle where a huge diamond and a matching Verdonia Royal were connected in a swirl of gold.

What had Lander said about the Blushes? That they symbolized a contract. Wasn't that how their engagement had begun, as a contract? She might have been unaware of it, but that didn't make it any less true. She frowned in concentration. The Blushes were only on the outer rim. As they grew in size, they also changed to an unusual reddish-purple color that was neither Blush nor Royal. She wasn't sure what this new shade symbolized. None of the jewels Lander had shown her had contained anything similar. But at the center of the ring the stones were the deepest, richest purple-blue she'd ever seen. A diamond and a Royal mated together. She shook her head. No. It couldn't possibly mean what she thought.

The tears came then, tears of regret mixed with a surge of hope so expansive and strong that it drowned out every other emotion. It took two circuits around the block before she'd recovered sufficiently to decide on her next step. Fumbling for her cell phone, she punched in a number. Her brother answered on the first ring.

"I need three things from you and I need them an hour ago," she announced.

"Name them and they're yours."

"I need your jet. My old team of accountants. And the meanest, nastiest, sharkiest bunch of lawyers you have on staff. I want to be airborne before nightfall."

"Going somewhere?"

"Verdonia."

Joc let out a sigh of relief. "About damn time."

"Lander! Lander, where are you going?" Rachel called breathlessly.

He paused, his hand on the knob of the conference room door, and glanced over his shoulder at his step-mother. To his surprise, she approached at a near run, alarm clear in her eyes. "I'm checking in with my lawyers and accountants, of course. I've called down at least six times today for an update and haven't heard a word."

"Maybe if you left them alone so they could get some work done—"

"This will only take a minute."

He pushed open the door and stepped into the room. Everyone froze, and the animated conversation came to an abrupt stop at his entry. And that's when he heard it, a soft gasp. He knew that tiny hiccup of sound, had heard it every time he'd kissed his wife, every time he'd made love to her, every time he'd brought her to completion. Slowly he turned his head and there she was, standing off to one side of the room, staring at him.

Of course her eyes gave her away, brilliant flecks of gold burning within the honey brown. He flinched at what he read there. Apprehension, longing, wariness. Even a heartrending hint of sorrow. But worst of all was the unadulterated pain.

He didn't hesitate. He was beside her in an instant. Cupping the back of her neck, he tumbled her into his arms. His mouth took hers with an intense kiss that told her more clearly than words how much he missed her. His tongue breached her lips and she responded to him the way she always did, with a generous passion that threatened to unman him. She wore her hair up in a style similar to the one on their wedding day, and he thrust his hands into those perfectly arranged curls and set them free.

At long last he pulled back and gazed down at her. "You're here."

"Yes, I'm here," she agreed breathlessly.

"Don't take this the wrong way, but…why?"

"I thought I could help."

Help. She meant help with the embezzling charges. Damn it! If the media got wind of her presence they'd be all over her. If she thought her previous experiences had been bad, it would be nothing compared to this. And there wouldn't be anything he could do to protect her. "I left specific instructions with Joc—"

"Yes," she cut in. "I heard those instructions, remember?"

Hell. Lander thrust a hand through his hair. "We need to take this someplace private where we can talk." He started to urge her from the room, only to discover that they were already alone. He paused, tempted to carry her off to their rooms while no one was watching and allow his hands and mouth to do his speaking for him. Duty battled desire for supremacy. Duty won. "You shouldn't be in Verdonia. You need to leave before word leaks of your return."

"I'm not going anywhere. At least, not yet." She stepped away from him and folded her arms across her chest. "Why didn't you tell me about these charges you're facing?"

"You left, remember?"

Hot color scorched her cheeks. "Vividly. I also remember the reason I left."

"And still you came back?" he couldn't help but ask. He didn't understand it. After everything he'd done to drive her away, here she stood.

She waved that aside as though it weren't important. "Why did you tell Joc to keep me out of Verdonia?" she countered. "Was it to protect me?"

He shrugged. "You've had enough trouble with the media to last a lifetime. You don't need any more."

"Falling on your sword, Lander?"

He managed a brief smile. "We seem to make a habit of it, don't we?" His smile faded. "Not that it matters. You're returning to Texas right now, even if I have to put you on the plane in handcuffs."

"Just one last question before I go." She hesitated before rushing into speech. "I couldn't help noticing that all the Verdonian wedding rings you showed me at the museum had names. Does mine?"

The change of topic caught him off guard and he answered automatically. "Of course."

"What is it?"

He should have seen the question coming and diverted her before she could ask. "We can discuss this later." He attempted to dismiss the subject. "The plane—"

"Can wait." One look warned she wouldn't be budged from her stance. "If you want my cooperation, we'll discuss it now."

He made the best of a losing hand. "If I tell you the name, do you agree to leave? To get on whatever plane brought you here and return to Texas within the hour?" At her nod, he bit out, "Metamorphous. Your ring is called Metamorphous."

"Ah." A strange smile tugged at her mouth. "I'd hoped it was something like that."

He started for the door. "If we're careful, I think I can get you to the airport with no one the wiser."

"In a minute." She laced his hand in hers and tugged him toward the conference table where papers were piled high. "I want to show you something first."

"We had an agreement, Juliana." Determination filled

him. This time he wouldn't fail. If she didn't come soon, he'd take more drastic action. Whatever necessary, so long as he protected her. "You promised you'd leave."

"I'll be quick." She shoved her loosened curls back from her face. "Normally I wouldn't allow a client in here while I'm working."

She was chattering from nerves, and his eyes narrowed as he watched her. "I'm not your client."

"It wouldn't matter if you were, not anymore." She edged around the table away from him and gathered up a sheaf of papers. Tidying them, she reached for another. "I'm through with my investigation."

He took the comment with calm stoicism. "Don't let it worry you. I know you did your best. Now if you don't mind—"

"I always do my best." And she smiled at him.

He saw it then. The quiet satisfaction. The breathtaking radiance that eased the lines of strain from his wife's face. "You figured out what happened to the amethysts," he marveled.

"Yes. Lauren DeVida happened to them."

"Our chief executive accountant?" He couldn't disguise his shock. "Not a chance in hell. She was devoted to my father. Devoted to Verdonia."

"No, she was pretty much devoted to stealing amethysts. I have to admit, she was good at it," Juliana reluctantly conceded. "She was really good."

"But not as good as you." There wasn't a doubt in his mind.

She struggled to appear modest. "No one's that good."

He sat down across from her. "Are you sure it was Lauren?"

"Sure enough that the accountants are reporting to

the Temporary Governing Council as we speak." She reached out and squeezed his hand. "She was like family, wasn't she?"

"Yes. My father adored her. We all did."

"Huh." Juliana's brows pulled together in thought. "I hadn't considered that possibility."

"What possibility?"

She riffled through some of the documents. "When were your father and Rachel married?" She flicked a piece of paper across the table toward him. "Was it around about this date?"

"Not around. Exactly."

"That's when the scam began. It ended the day your father died."

Damn it to hell. What had Juliana once said? One plus one always equals two. "You think Lauren was in love with my father, don't you?"

She nodded. "And when he married Rachel, that adoration turned vindictive. From what I've been able to uncover, she set up the entire operation to make it appear that your father, you and Merrick had run it. There are even documents that implicate Rachel and Miri. I'm guessing she sent copies of some of this to certain interested parties."

"Von Folke."

"It's possible. I haven't found any proof of that."

Lander glanced around the room, taking in the controlled chaos. "What's left for you to do here?"

"Nothing. As soon as we let everyone back in, copies will be made. Reports written." She shrugged. "Details finalized."

"You're certain? There's no question that it's finished?"

"I'm positive."

"That leaves one last task for me to deal with." Without warning, he circled the conference table and swept her up into his arms.

She released a muffled cry. "What do you think you're doing?"

"I'm taking a page out of Merrick's book."

"I...I don't understand." A heartbreaking ache underscored her words. "Are you still sending me home? I know I promised to go, but—"

"I'm abducting you, not sending you home," he explained gravely. "It worked so well for Merrick that I thought I'd give it a try."

"You're going to—"

He silenced her with a kiss. When he came up for air again, he said, "Abduct you. Yes. Would you prefer to be tied up?"

"That won't be necessary." Looping her hands around his neck she released a disgruntled sigh. "It would seem I don't have a choice." She peeked up at him, her eyes shining like burnished gold. "Do I?"

"You can fight. But I recommend cooperation. That way you don't invalidate Section C, Subparagraph Four, Line Sixteen of my contract with Joc."

She stiffened within his hold. "Dare I ask?"

"I believe it has to do with love, honor and cherish until death do us part."

Something shifted in her expression, a slow undoing, a helpless breaking signaling the final release of a lifetime's worth of barriers. Without a word, she closed her eyes and lowered her head to his shoulder. He carried her from the room. In no time he had a limo arranged to transport them to the apartment building where he'd first made love to his wife.

"I should have sent Joc packing the minute he proposed that outrageous contract," he told her, once they were inside.

"Why didn't you?"

"Verdonia," he said simply. "And then later, there was no reason to terminate our agreement. Why would I? It gave me everything I wanted." He reached for her. Now that she'd returned, he couldn't seem to keep his hands off her. "It gave me you."

"Oh, Lander." She clung to him. "You should have told me you were in trouble sooner," she informed him fiercely. "I would have been on the next plane back to you. We could have had this resolved a week ago."

It was all he needed to hear. She lifted her face to his kiss at the same instant as he lowered his. Their mouths collided, setting the mating dance into motion. Clothes were shed with overwhelming haste. Limbs entwined. And then they were on the bed, with nothing between them but a desperate urgency.

They surged together, the crest building, the subtle upheaval like waves fomenting before a distant storm. Juliana undulated beneath him, arching into the ebb and flow of their mating, the depth and intensity increasing before the steady advance of the tempest. And then it was on top of them, breaking loose from all restraint. Crashing and clawing at emotions drawn bow-string taut. Howling for release. They were swept high into the storm's embrace, and in that instant, she came undone, shattering in his arms.

Lander watched her, reveling in the knowledge that he'd brought her to crisis. Humbled by the fact that his hands, his mouth, his body, his touch—and his alone— could cause such an intense climax. The storm lashed out with a final violent kick. Roaring through him. Furious. Wrenching. And he followed her into the very heart of it, clinging to the one person in the universe who completed him. Who sheltered and fulfilled him.

His bride. His princess. His wife.

Much later, Lander rolled onto his back and scooped Juliana tight against him. By then dusk had settled in, leaving the room in semidarkness. He slid his fingers into her hair, filling his hands with her curls. He experienced a loosening deep inside, the knowledge that his world would only be right when it was like this—with his wife in his arms and his hands on her.

"Why did you return?" he felt compelled to ask.

Her calm gaze remained fixed on his, filled with an absolute certainty. "I returned because I realized you loved me as much as I loved you."

His brows drew together. "Of course I love you."

"You never said the words," she replied simply.

Hell. How could he have overlooked something so obvious? "Then how did you know?"

"The wedding rings. I'd forgotten what you'd told me on our wedding day, about their having a special meaning. But then Rachel reminded me." Her voice softened, grew richer. "That's when I put it all together."

"What did you put together?"

"That you loved me." She held up her hand, her rings giving off a subdued flash of fire. "The Blushes on the outside represent how our relationship began, as part of a contract. But then the stones change and grow, just as our feelings for each other changed and grew. At the very heart, it's a metamorphous from contract to soul mate."

"I couldn't have put it better myself." He smoothed

her hair away from her face. "I love you, Juliana. I have for a long time. But I knew you wouldn't believe words alone. They're too easy."

"Even so, you put the words in the ring. I found those, too. In the gold filigree. It says 'true love' in Verdonian. There's only one thing I don't understand."

"And what's that?"

She ran her fingertip over the stones set between the Blushes and Royals. "The meaning of these other amethysts. The ones between the pink and purple. They're such a unique color. Not quite red, not quite blue, nor purple. Yet, all of them mixed together. I've never seen an amethyst quite like it."

"My father came across the stones years ago. Apparently just these few were coughed out of the mines. Nothing like them has been found since."

"They're so distinctive."

"So is their name."

"Really?" She looked up at him, innocent curiosity reflected in her face. "What are they called?"

He stroked her ring, touching each stone in turn. "The Celestia Blush. The sealing of a contract. The Verdonia Royal. To represent soul mates." His finger lingered on the final group of stones. "And these were named by royal proclamation on our wedding day. This color is now known as the Juliana Rose, and will forever after symbolize true love."

She wept then, helpless tears of disbelief and joy. He held her patiently until they'd eased. Wiping the dampness from her cheeks, she wound her arms around his neck. Her eyes shone brighter than the sun as she kissed him three times, each deeper and more passionate than the last. The first kiss sealed their marriage contract. The second was reserved for soul mates. And finally, she gave him the kiss of true love.

"You should know that you've done something for me no one else has ever been able to do," she whispered against his mouth.

"What's that, Princess?"

She laughed away the last of her tears. "You've made all my dreams come true."

He smiled contentedly. "Now that sounds like the perfect job for a prince."

* * * * *

Day Leclaire's THE ROYALS *series
continues next month.
Don't miss THE ROYAL WEDDING NIGHT,
available in April from Silhouette Desire.*

Turn the page for a sneak preview of
IF I'D NEVER KNOWN YOUR LOVE
by
Georgia Bockoven

From the brand-new series
Harlequin Everlasting Love
Every great love has a story to tell. ™

One year, five months and four days missing

There's no way for you to know this, Evan, but I haven't written to you for a few months. Actually, it's been almost a year. I had a hard time picking up a pen once more after we paid the second ransom and then received a letter saying it wasn't enough. I was so sure you were coming home that I took the kids along to Bogotá so they could fly home with you and me, something I swore I'd never do. I've fallen in love with Colombia and the people who've opened their hearts to me. But fear is a constant companion when I'm there. I won't ever expose our children to that kind of danger again.

I'm at a loss over what to do anymore, Evan. I've begged and pleaded and thrown temper tantrums with every official I can corner both here and at home. They've been incredibly tolerant and understanding, but in the end as ineffectual as the rest of us.

I try to imagine what your life is like now, what you do every day, what you're wearing, what you eat. I want to believe that the people who have you are misguided yet kind, that they treat you well. It's how I survive day to day. To think of you being mistreated hurts too much. If I picture you locked away somewhere and suffering, a weight descends on me that makes it almost impossible to get out of bed in the morning.

Your captors surely know you by now. They have to recognize what a good man you are. I imagine you working with their children, telling them that you have children, too, showing them the pictures you carry in your wallet. Can't the men who have you understand how much your children miss you? How can it not matter to them?

How can they keep you away from us all this time? Over and over, we've done what they asked. Are they oblivious to the depth of their cruelty? What kind of people are they that they don't care?

I used to keep a calendar beside our bed next to the peach rose you picked for me before you left. Every night I marked another day, counting how many you'd been gone. I don't do that any longer. I don't want to be reminded of all the days we'll never get back.

When I can't sleep at night, I tell you about my day. I imagine you hearing me and smiling over the details that make up my life now. I never tell you how defeated I feel at moments or how hard I work to hide it from everyone for fear they will see it as a reason to stop believing you are coming home to us.

And I couldn't tell you about the lump I found in my breast and how difficult it was going through all the tests without you here to lean on. The lump was benign—the process reaching that diagnosis utterly terrifying. I couldn't stop thinking about what would happen to Shelly and Jason if something happened to me.

We need you to come home.

I'm worn down with missing you.

I'm going to read this tomorrow and will probably tear it up or burn it in the fireplace. I don't want you to get the idea I ever doubted what I was doing to free you or thought the work a burden. I would gladly spend the rest of my life at it, even if, in the end, we only had one day together.

You are my life, Evan.

I will love you forever.

* * * * *

*Don't miss this deeply moving
Harlequin Everlasting Love story about a woman's
struggle to bring back her kidnapped husband from
Colombia and her turmoil over whether to let go,
finally, and welcome another man into her life.
IF I'D NEVER KNOWN YOUR LOVE
by Georgia Bockoven
is available March 27, 2007.*

*And also look for
THE NIGHT WE MET
by Tara Taylor Quinn,
a story about finding love
when you least expect it.*

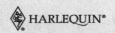

REQUEST YOUR FREE BOOKS!

2 FREE NOVELS
PLUS 2
FREE GIFTS!

Passionate, Powerful, Provocative!

SDES07

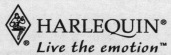

Silhouette Desire

Introducing talented new author

TESSA RADLEY

*making her Silhouette Desire debut
this April with*

BLACK WIDOW BRIDE

Book #1794
Available in April 2007.

Wealthy Damon Asteriades had no choice but to
force Rebecca Grainger back to his family's estate—
despite his vow to keep away from her seductive
charms. But being so close to the woman society once
dubbed the Black Widow Bride had him aching to
claim her as his own...at any cost.

On sale April from Silhouette Desire!

**Available wherever books are sold,
including most bookstores, supermarkets,
discount stores and drugstores.**

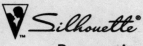

COMING NEXT MONTH

#1789 MISTRESS OF FORTUNE—Kathie DeNosky
Dakota Fortunes
A casino magnate seeks revenge on his family by seducing his brother's stunning companion and daring her to become Fortune's mistress.

#1790 BLACKHAWK'S AFFAIR—Barbara McCauley
Secrets!
What's a woman to do when she comes face-to-face with the man who broke her heart years before…and realizes he's still her husband?

#1791 HER FORBIDDEN FIANCÉE—Christie Ridgway
Millionaire of the Month
He'd been mistaken for his identical twin before—but now his estranged sibling's lovely fiancée believes he's the man she wants to sleep with.

#1792 THE ROYAL WEDDING NIGHT—Day Leclaire
The Royals
Deceived at the altar, a prince sleeps with the wrong bride. But after sharing the royal wedding night with his mystery woman, nothing will stop him from discovering who she really is.

#1793 THE BILLIONAIRE'S BIDDING—Barbara Dunlop
A hotel heiress vows to save her family's business from financial ruin at any cost. Then she discovers the price is marrying her enemy.

#1794 BLACK WIDOW BRIDE—Tessa Radley
He despised her. He desired her. And the billionaire was just desperate enough to blackmail her back into his life.

SDCNM0307